Y0-AQR-764

THE
HOUSEBOAT
MYSTERY

THE HOUSEBOAT MYSTERY

Jane Edwards

A
c.1

Thorndike Press • Chivers Press
Thorndike, Maine USA   Bath, England

This Large Print edition is published by Thorndike Press, USA and by Chivers Press, England.

Published in 1999 in the U.S. by arrangement with Jane Edwards.

Published in 1999 in the U.K. by arrangement with the author.

U.S. Hardcover 0-7862-1875-4 (Candlelight Series Edition)
U.K. Hardcover 0-7540-3759-2 (Chivers Large Print)

The text of this Large Print edition is unabridged.
Other aspects of the book may vary from the original edition.

Set in 16 pt. Plantin by Rick Gundberg.

Printed in the United States on permanent paper.

British Library Cataloguing in Publication Data available

Library of Congress Cataloging in Publication Data

Edwards, Jane (Jane Campbell), 1932–
    The houseboat mystery / Jane Edwards.
      p.   cm.
    ISBN 0-7862-1875-4 (lg. print : hc : alk. paper)
    1. Large type books. I. Title.
    [PS3555.D933H68   1999]
    813'.54—dc21   99-11206

For My Uncle
REV. GEORGE A. CAMPBELL
In Gratitude and Affection

CHAPTER ONE

Jackie Torrance wasn't looking for trouble that bright Thursday morning late in June. All she really wanted to do was to find a place to live.

"I can't," she told herself practically, "go on bunking with Val forever."

In less than a month Val would no longer be dear, familiar Valerie Prescott, but Mrs. Gregory Malden. Jackie would, of course, remain a part of the Prescott household until after the wedding, but then, with Val honeymooning and her parents away in Europe on a vacation, she would simply *have* to find an apartment of her own. Either that or go back to Los Angeles.

And I don't want to, she thought. Sometimes I think I don't ever want to leave Santa Teresa again.

It felt so good to be home at last. Her hairbrush poised in mid-air, Jackie let her eyes stray to the bedroom window, and beyond. The twining, fragrant jasmine, the trees tiptoeing down the slope to the inlet . . .

Such a long two years it had been! Two years spent in Los Angeles after her father's promotion and transfer to the head office of his insurance company there. Now, back in Santa Teresa for the first time since her graduation from high school, Jackie realized how very much she had missed the friendly hominess of the little seacoast town.

She would have to leave in September, of course — if she decided to return to college. But September just now seemed light years away, and in the meantime, she had three glorious months —

Three glorious months without a job if I don't get a move on!

She cast a horrified look at the clock and snatched up the crisp linen jacket of her suit. Clattering at breakneck speed down the stairs, she caught up with Val on the landing.

Although they had been close friends since childhood, the two girls could hardly have been more dissimilar in appearance. Jackie's short dark hair was brushed into a glossy cap ending smoothly at her earlobes, Val's blonde pageboy curled about her shoulders; Jackie's eyes were a lively brown, Val's a lark-spur blue; Jackie, even without her high heels was tall, while Val and the yardstick met head on at five feet one.

"Don't rush," Val told her. "Dad has to go downtown this morning. He'll drop you off at the *Courier* building."

"Deluxe! I've been upstairs daydreaming, and the clock sort of got ahead of me," Jackie confessed as they seated themselves at the table with Mr. and Mrs. Prescott.

Chatting companionably, they devoured a delicious breakfast of hotcakes and bacon.

"Is your job still holding its fascination, Jackie?" Mr. Prescott asked presently. "Or shall I remind Bruce MacFarland that it's time you had a raise?"

"After only two weeks? We'd better give him a chance to realize who I am first." Jackie laughed. The *Courier*'s Editor had little personal contact with his fledgling reporters. "Actually, I catch only blurred glimpses of him whizzing in and out of the City Room. He has wished me off on the Society Department, so Melinda Foster is my immediate boss. She's fun, and easy to work with."

"Fun or not, please don't get involved with any committee women tonight," Val implored. "Remember that bushel of invitations hanging over our heads. If we don't get them addressed soon —"

"Relax! I'll be home at the stroke of six with my fountain pen aquiver," Jackie promised.

She shrugged into her jacket and followed

Mr. Prescott out to the car, still thinking of her newly acquired job on the paper. Working for the *Courier* was a Cloud Nine dream come true — a dream which might never have been fulfilled were it not for Mr. Prescott's friendship with Editor MacFarland. Without the promise of employment in Santa Teresa, she would have been unable to accept Val's invitation to spend the six weeks before the wedding as her guest and prospective maid of honor. She was determined to prove that her ability measured up to the confidence which had been placed in her.

As usual, the Courier Building hummed with activity. This morning, though, Jackie noted with a puzzled frown, the hum was subdued and the activity, instead of centering on the clack of high-tech machinery and the shrilling telephones in the advertising booths, revolved around the newspaper personnel. Employees clustered together in murmuring knots. Even as she watched, they spilled apart and quickly regrouped into new little clusters. The almost rhythmic flow reminded her of a game of musical chairs.

Looks as if something really gossip-worthy has happened, she decided.

The elevator operator scarcely glanced at her. Without a word, he pressed the button that would lift the cage to the fourth floor, and returned to an absorbed perusal of the newspaper in his hand.

"Can't believe it," Jackie heard him mutter as the door clanged open.

What couldn't he believe? The question had almost crossed her lips before she bit it back. If anything devastating enough to shake the *Courier* plant to its very elevators had occurred, Melinda Foster would know about it. Melinda always seemed to know everything — scandals, secrets, good news and bad always appeared to reach her desk before anyone else had an inkling of the details.

But one look at the Society Editor's tear-streaked face warned Jackie that whatever the excitement concerned, it had nothing to do with scandals or secrets.

"Melinda!" she exclaimed. "What's going on around here?"

"He's dead," Melinda said, in a flat, dull voice.

Jackie stared. "Who?"

A flash of exasperation heated Melinda's reddened eyes. She thrust a morning edition of the *Courier* into the younger girl's hands. "You work on a newspaper and don't even read it?"

"There wasn't time this morning. I was —" Jackie broke off, gaping incredulously at the banner headline splashed across the page.

11

"Lance Shelby? Oh, no!"

She sank into the nearest chair. Word had arrived late last night, the article screamed, that the *Courier*'s ace reporter, Lance Shelby, was aboard the British airliner en route from Hong Kong to Honolulu which had crashed into the sea a few minutes after take-off. Shelby, whose by-line was internationally famous, had been returning to California after completion of an assignment in the Far East. A great loss.

"It — it's hard to believe," Jackie murmured, unconsciously echoing the elevator operator's sentiments.

She had known Lance Shelby only by sight, but once seen, he was not easily forgotten. Tall and dark and almost Hollywoodishly handsome, Shelby's ability to ferret out sensational "behind-the-scenes" aspects of stories which others had found purely routine was legendary. It seemed incredible that his vital, restless personality had been stilled forever.

Jackie glanced around the room. No wonder reporters and cameramen ignored their work, or that Melinda Foster, who had never made a secret of the tremendous crush she had on Lance, sat woodenly at her with a look of numb endurance on her face.

"The lounge ought to be deserted now,"

12

Jackie suggested. "Maybe a good hot cup of tea —" Or a good bawl, she added silently.

Melinda fumbled blindly for her purse and fled. Jackie logged on the appropriate computer program and began drafting the lead item for the "Neighborhood Notes" column which would appear in the next morning's *Courier*. By the time Melinda reappeared, a measure of composure restored to her lovely oval face, the column was blocked into shape and Jackie was running a final check on name spellings.

"All quiet on the Society front," she reported.

Melinda's smile was wobbly, but determined. "Thanks. Find Don, will you, and ask him when the Willard photos will be ready. I must have them by noon, or they won't make the Sunday women's section deadline."

Jackie sped downstairs to the photographic department.

"Hot off the negatives," Don George, one of the junior cameramen, said. He slipped the prints into an envelope. "No panic-button problems in Society? How's Melinda taking the news about Shelby?"

"Hard," Jackie admitted. "I imagine everyone was pretty much shocked."

Ted Rigney came out of the darkroom drying his hands. "Tough break for Lance," he said. "Wonder what will happen to all his stuff? He had no relatives in town that I know of."

"By tomorrow next-of-kins will be popping up all over the place," Don predicted. "I wouldn't be surprised if the police padlocked his apartment against souvenir hunters. Lance was awfully well known."

"Apartment?" Jackie perked up her ears. "I know it sounds ghoulish after — after what had just happened, but I've been looking for a place of my own."

"Listen to the girl!" Don hooted. "I take it you never saw Shelby's layout. The rent on that penthouse of his would have made Bill Gates say 'ouch.' "

"P-penthouse?"

"Maybe she'd be interested in taking over his houseboat," Ted said, with a wink at Don. "That is, if she doesn't mind the smell of fish."

Ted Rigney was noted for his practical jokes. "Who," Jackie asked suspiciously, "would pay two thousand dollars for a penthouse and then live on a houseboat?"

Ted chuckled. "I didn't say he lived on it. He used it week-ends for fishing trips. Not a bad old tub, either." He struck a pose. "Picture the romance of it. Gentle waves rocking the hammock as a mellow moon beams down

14

on the intrepid girl reporter —"

"— The one hanging over the side; she's seasick," Don broke in. "A storm has blown up! Now our luminous luna is cowering in a cloud bank. That moon isn't mellow; it's yellow! Ah, but does that daunt her? While typhoons splinter the mast, she carries on with her little paddle. Jacqueline Torrance, girl flash, must be at the *Courier* by eight bells, or the presses cannot roll!"

"Correction! Jacqueline Torrance, girl errand runner, must be back at her desk by eleven bells, or whatever is three minutes from now, or the pay check won't come through!"

Ignoring their raillery, Jackie tucked the envelope of prints under her arm and marched back up the stairs. A houseboat! Of all the moronic suggestions! Working girls simply didn't live on houseboats. Still, she conceded, interested in spite of herself, it sounded like fun.

The notion quickly vanished, however. Back on the fourth floor a clamoring telephone and an "in" basket swamped with mail took all her attention. Early in the afternoon, Melinda clapped her own flowered hat on Jackie's head and sent her off to cover a garden party, declaring that on this of all days she could not face Agnes Van Roth and

15

her gossipy circle of friends.

"What a day!" Jackie exclaimed, hobbling back to the comparative restfulness of the Prescott home.

"Bedlam?" Val asked sympathetically.

"Yes, though I wouldn't have phrased it so mildly. Between wringing out Melinda's hankies and assuring Mrs. Van Roth that all her guests at the garden party would have their names in the paper, I feel like a walking tranquilizer pill!"

Val nodded. "We read about Lance Shelby. I imagine the *Courier* was a real madhouse."

"It was." Jackie sighed. "I'm about to go and have a nice, noisy tantrum of my own!"

After clearing away the dinner dishes, she and Val tackled the stacks of engraved invitations which had arrived from the print shop a few days earlier.

"I can hardly wait to see Greg again," Jackie said enthusiastically, checking the last name off one list and reaching for another. "He was a couple of years ahead of us in school, but I'll never forget those touchdown passes he threw against Graham. I guess he had already entered the Navy by the time we moved to the city."

"Yes, we started dating on his first leave home," Val reminisced. "It all seems so long

16

ago. I can hardly believe that he'll be discharged tomorrow."

Greg's father was a successful real-estate broker in San Francisco now, and Val and Greg would make their home in that city after they were married. Jackie felt a tiny twinge of envy at her friend's good fortune. Would there come a time when she, too, would meet someone for whom she would be willing to move far away from family and friends? He would have to be very special. But Val obviously felt no doubts. To her, Greg was the most special person in the world.

"How many people are coming to this wedding, anyway?" Jackie asked when another hour had passed. The lists of guests to whom invitations still had to be addressed seemed endless.

Val confessed that she had lost count. "My folks, Greg's folks, Aunt Louise — they all come up with more names every day. We'll have to hold the ceremony in an auditorium if they don't run out of ideas soon."

It was past midnight before the last envelope was sealed and stamped. Congratulating themselves on still being able to flex their fingers, the girls plodded upstairs.

Jackie lingered an extra few minutes under the shower that night, slowly relaxing as the day's headaches gurgled down the drain with the suds. Tumbling into bed, it never occurred to her that those same headaches were only a prelude to the adventures and near-tragedy which were to come.

CHAPTER TWO

The next morning, Jackie was kept busy typing her notes on the Van Roth party and other social events, answering calls and making appointments for Melinda. After lunch, she settled down to a thorough reading of the *Courier* and the *Herald.* Both papers carried much the same news; it was only in the way the items were presented that the rival newspapers differed.

"The *Courier* states more facts, while the *Herald* emphasizes speculation and gossip," Jackie said aloud, wondering if perhaps this might account for the *Herald*'s larger circulation.

For purposes of comparison, she clipped an article from each paper. Each was basically the same, a discreetly worded release from the Naval authorities in Port Dixon that blueprints for a new atomic submarine had disappeared despite the rigid security precautions which had been enforced to protect them.

"The *Courier* leaves it at that; the *Herald*

adds three full paragraphs, hinting at every-thing from spies to subversion in the Armed Forces," Jackie commented, at the same time recalling that Port Dixon was the base at which Greg Malden was stationed. She turned to Melinda. "Do you really think all this sensationalism helps sell papers?"

"It must." Melinda shrugged. "Look at the *Herald*'s subscription total. It's twice the size of ours."

Jackie paged through to the want ads. As usual, there were no listings of apartments for rent in a price range which she could afford. Suddenly, a "Boats for Sale" column re-minded her of Ted Rigney's mirthful sugges-tion that she consider Lance Shelby's house-boat as a prospective home. Of course he had been clowning, but —

"Well, why not?" she asked herself. "It wouldn't cost anything to take a look at it. If I moored it in that little inlet down by Val's house, I'd be just a few blocks from the bus and the supermarket. There might be some other advantages, too."

Impulsively, she dialed Ted's extension.

"You're not serious!" he exclaimed, appalled at her question. "Can't you tell when a fellow is joking?"

"The idea grew on me overnight," Jackie told him. "I got to thinking how glorious it would be never having to bother with door-to-door salesmen. I could just haul up the gangplank, or whatever it is houseboats have, and nobody could pester me."

"You'd see how glorious it was the first time a storm blew up!"

"You're talking to a girl who practically teethed on a sailboat. Come on. All I'm asking is where Lance Shelby kept this seagoing palace."

"Tied up at Dodson's Dockyard," Ted answered, with a sigh of resignation. "But I still don't think —"

"Thanks, Ted," she said quickly. "You're a dear. I'll invite you over to snap pictures of me charting a course on the bridge."

"Jackie Torrance, girl nut!" she heard him sputter before breaking the connection.

She phoned Val to say that she wouldn't be home for dinner, and sprinted for the bus stop at the first blare of the five o'clock whistle.

Picking her way along the warped wooden boardwalk which fronted the harbor, she felt a tingle of excitement. Soon, though, doubt crept in to replace her optimism.

There was nothing remotely resembling a houseboat at any of the piers she passed. Supposing Ted had invented the whole thing? He would probably have considered it hilarious to send her dashing off to hunt for an imaginary houseboat.

Just about the time she had convinced herself that she had fallen for one of the cameraman's practical jokes, Jackie spotted a Quonset-hut type building with the word "Dodson" painted in wavery letters across its corrugated side.

I've come this far. Might as well let everyone have a good laugh at my expense, she decided after a moment's hesitation.

To her surprise, the dock-keeper seemed to find nothing peculiar in her inquiry.

"Yup," he said, "I've got a houseboat. Rent her or buy her, all the same to me. Newspaper feller had her for a spell, but from what I hear, he won't be needing her any more. His rent was up, anyhow."

"Where is — Could I take a look at it — her?" Jackie asked, sending a mental apology to Ted Rigney.

"Pier Six, but just follow the crowd," Mr. Dodson told her. "My boy Chuck is down there now. He'll show you around, and if you decide you want her, he can make out a receipt." He squinted, staring frankly at her, his expression one of puzzled suspicion. "Young lady, you're the fourth person to ask about that houseboat in the last hour. Most interest folks have taken in a boat of mine in twenty years. Seems a mite peculiar."

22

Jackie thanked him and left the Quonset hut feeling slightly perplexed. "A mite peculiar" was right. Why this sudden demand for secondhand houseboats? She had thought her own inspiration about renting it unique. Now it appeared that half the town had had a similar idea.

I'm certain the houseboat wasn't advertised in either paper, she thought, recalling her thorough search of the want ads. I wonder how everyone else found out it was available?

Within a short time, she caught sight of an unwieldy vessel bumping alongside the dock. It floated low in the water, and its prow kept nosing outward as if the dingy old boat were ashamed of its blistered, peeling paint and unkempt decks.

Climbing aboard, Jackie felt her hopes sag. Back at her desk the idea of leading a carefree existence anchored in a snug little bay had seemed the merriest of larks. She realized now that her knowledge of houseboats was sadly deficient. A wide gap existed between the spic-and-span, yachtlike craft she had visualized and the shabby reality she now set about exploring.

But the decks were spacious, if splintery, and the sturdy trio of cabins built along the vessel's mid-section were airy and well lighted. Still reluctant to admit that her "inspiration" had been a complete fizzle, Jackie decided that a glimpse of the interior might change her mind about the unsuitability of the houseboat.

The three cabins were placed end to end, like the rooms of an old-fashioned "shotgun" house. Stepping into the first cabin, Jackie heard quarreling voices raised nearby. She was too much engrossed by her inspection tour, however, to pay much attention.

"This isn't bad at all," she murmured.

Bunks were clamped securely to the wall — bulkhead, she supposed it was called — between a pair of sturdy sea chests. Several comfortable chairs were placed conveniently around the colorful matting which served as a rug. There were even a few framed sporting prints hung casually alongside the portholes.

Agreeably impressed by what she had seen so far, Jackie pulled open the door to the middle cabin — and stepped into the midst of a loud argument.

Four men stood practically toe to toe in the center of the room. Startled, she found herself a witness to their angry discussion.

"I'm sorry," an apologetic-looking youth was saying, obviously not for the first time. Jackie guessed that this must be Chuck, the dockman's son. "I told you these fellows were here first. We've already signed an agreement."

"Money is no object," the stolid, rumple-suited man whom he had addressed growled obstinately. "Name your price. I will meet it."

"It's no deal, mister," a tall, redheaded young man in a Naval uniform said. He waved what appeared to be a bill of sale. "We came, we liked, we bought. Find yourself another houseboat."

"I have found the houseboat I want." The man was mulishly insistent. "How much have you paid? Six thousand? I will give ten thousand — four thousand dollars' clear profit for you and your friend."

"Look, if you want to play Santa Claus in June, that's your business," the redheaded sailor declared. "I don't like to be rude, but you have lost this engagement. You've been torpedoed, depth charged, scuttled!"

Jackie, a fascinated spectator, moved hastily out of the doorway as the heavy-jowled man in the wrinkled brown suit stalked past her. His beetling brows were drawn together in a black scowl, and on his glowering face was one of the most vindictive expressions she had ever seen. She didn't envy the house-boat's new owner one bit. He had won this particular skirmish, but she instinctively felt that in doing so he had also gained a dangerous adversary.

"We have met the enemy and they are ours . . ." the redhead quoted with a grin.

"I'm afraid he has not yet begun to fight," warned the blond lieutenant, whose face Jackie could not see. "He looked like a pirate to me, Whit. Better watch yourself in dark alleys."

"Oh, I think we spiked his guns. But what a persistent character!" Whit stooped to shoulder his duffel bag. Straightening up, he caught sight of Jackie.

"Welcome aboard," he called, adding a complimentary whistle. "If we had twenty-one guns —"

Jackie, belatedly aware that she had been trespassing, eavesdropping, and committing heaven knew how many other misdemeanors, blushed and edged backwards. An instant later, she suddenly halted. The blond lieutenant had about-faced at his friend's words, and she stared at him in open-mouthed astonishment.

"Why, Greg Malden!" she gasped. "What are *you* doing here?"

Greg looked blank for a moment. Then, as her identity dawned on him, he strode forward to take her hands in a warm clasp.

"Jackie Torrance! Say, how did you know

I'd be here? Val wrote that you were staying with her, but I hardly expected you to form a reception committee." He held her at arms' length for a more thorough scrutiny. "You've grown up!"

"That's what I keep telling my parents," she said, laughing.

Chuck Dodson broke into a relieved smile. "I'm mighty glad you two are friends!" he exclaimed. "For a while there, I was afraid you were another customer wanting to buy the *Albatross*."

"Well, I was, almost," Jackie confessed. "But from what I've seen, I guess I arrived latest with the leastest."

"You wouldn't have liked the competition," the other sailor declared after Greg had performed the introductions and identified him as Whitney Egan. He turned to Chuck. "Who was our snarling competitor, anyway?"

"He gave his name as Smith," Chuck said dubiously.

Jackie sniffed. "With an accent like that, it would more likely be Smithovitch. Did he say why he was so eager to buy this particular houseboat?"

Whit shook his head. "Nope. Just sailed in here prepared to hoist anchor. He tried some 'you'll-be-sorry-if-you-don't' tactics on us first, and when he found we didn't scare

27

easily, he started waving his wallet. By that time, I was so mad I wouldn't have sold for fifty thousand!"

"It seems awfully peculiar. Not that this isn't a nice houseboat," Jackie hastened to add. "But Mr. Dodson mentioned that I was the fourth person to inquire about it in the last hour. I suppose he meant Mr. Smith, you and Greg, and myself."

"There was someone else, too," Chuck put in. "He telephoned yesterday and a couple of times today, insisting that we hold off selling the *Albatross* until he got here. Pa told him first come, first served, but he didn't seem to get discouraged very easily."

"Maybe that was our mysterious Mr. Smith," Greg suggested.

"The fellow on the phone had a Southern drawl," Chuck said flatly. He shrugged, glad to be rid of the problem. Descending to the wharf, he informed Whit that he could take possession of the houseboat that evening, since it would require only a few hours to remove the former owner's possessions to a storage room.

"I'd better call Val," Jackie said suddenly. "She would never forgive me if I let you catch her in curlers, Greg. We weren't expecting you until tomorrow."

Her phone call completed, she and Whit

Egan piled into Greg's shiny new convertible. "What do you intend to do with the houseboat, now that you've bought her?" she asked Whit.

"Turn her into a restaurant." He grinned. "Sound silly? You'd be surprised at how many chefs ladle up their soup in old railway cars and streetcars. This should be quite a novelty in Santa Teresa — I'll bet we won't have room for half the people who will line up for a seagoing sirloin once we swab down the decks and freshen up her paint."

Jackie smiled at his enthusiasm. "It sounds like a wonderful idea! One thing puzzles me, though. How did you discover that this particular houseboat was for sale?"

"Lucky accident. I was waiting outside a phone booth near the base yesterday and I overheard this guy inside mention a houseboat at Dodson's in Santa Teresa. I didn't see his face — but he sounded like he was going to talk all day so I went to buy a newspaper. When I came back, he was gone."

"Whit's been dreaming about owning a houseboat ever since we ate at a place called 'The Willows' in Honolulu," Greg put in. "It's a fantastic spot, built like a huge raft over a pond. You can even pick out your own frog legs there."

Jackie wrinkled her nose, but before she

29

could reply, Greg had leaped out and was halfway up the front steps of the Prescott house. She and Whit discreetly delayed their exit from the car for a few minutes, then joined the engaged couple.

"You *would* have to show up tonight!" Val was saying, although she was smiling happily. "This is Mother's evening for volunteer work at the hospital, and Dad has gone bowling with his League. When Jackie called to say she wouldn't be home either, I decided to make myself a sandwich. I haven't a thing pre-pared!"

"Point me in the direction of the kitchen," Whit said. "This likely looking K.P. assistant and I will stir up a few calories while you two hold hands."

No one objected, and half an hour later, after selecting various items from the pantry shelves, Whit had a salmon souffle puffing in the oven and was measuring ingredients for the lemon sauce which was to accompany it.

"Where did you learn to cook?" Jackie asked him, rinsing salad greens under the faucet.

"On our ranch in Montana. Mom gave up hoping for a girl after six boys and recruited the baby of the family to help her feed the threshers. Once you have cooked for threshers," Whit added emphatically, "feeding

30

cabins, then they all stretched out on canvas deck chairs while Whit outlined his plans for the refurbishment of the boat. A former ship-mate, he explained, would go into partnership with him when his discharge came through in about two weeks.

"We'll spot tables all along the port and starboard decks," he said. "Should be able to fit fifteen on each side without crowding. I'd like to raise a small stage at the stern there — maybe hire an accordionist to keep the customers happy."

"What about the cabins?" Val asked. "Will you turn them into dining rooms, too?"

"Not at first — at least, not until we see how business goes. We'll just keep them as living quarters and expand the galley to —" Whit broke off and strode over to the rail.

"Seasick — after two years of destroyer duty?" Greg hooted.

"That's the second time that car has driven past here." Whit frowned, staring after a pair of rapidly disappearing taillights along the bend of the water front.

"Same car? So what? Maybe they like the view," Greg said offhandedly.

"Maybe."

"You don't think it might have been that dreadful Mr. Smith, do you?" Jackie asked.

A sober expression had settled over Whit's

face. "No, it wasn't Santa Claus. I got a fair look at the driver the second time he cruised by. It could have been Buck Younger."

Jackie and Val exchanged puzzled glances. The name meant nothing to them.

"Your twenty-twenty is going back on you, pal," Greg scoffed. "Younger must be a thousand miles away from here by this time. A guy doesn't crash out of the brig and then hang around playing tag with the Shore Patrol."

"Younger is a Texan," Whit recalled, rubbing his chin. "Now that I think about it, the voice in that phone booth did have a pronounced drawl. *And,*" he added, "the person who phoned the Dodsons *also* had a drawl."

"Coincidence," declared Greg. Nevertheless, he seemed a bit disconcerted. "Look, Whit — Younger hated every second he spent in the Navy. Why should he hang around the water now, when he could be down in Waco rustling steers?"

Whit had no answer to that. He merely repeated that there were some coincidences that even Jonah's whale would have trouble swallowing.

"Who is Buck Younger?" Jackie asked, her curiosity piqued.

"Fellow we knew in Port Dixon. He fought," Greg said briefly.

"Brawled," Whit corrected. "Not the sort

34

of character you'd bring home to meet Mother."

"Or even Father," Greg said with finality, and the conversation swung to a more pleasant topic.

It was decided that Jackie and Val should drive home in Greg's car while Greg and Whit remained aboard the houseboat overnight.

"I want to talk to Mr. Dodson again first thing in the morning. He's to transfer all the papers for the *Albatross* to me then," Whit said.

It was a reasonable explanation — but after a look at his set expression, Jackie guessed that he intended to batten down the hatches and stand by ready to repel boarders.

"He could do it, too," she told herself. Somehow she felt as if her acquaintanceship with Whit had spanned months, instead of one short evening.

I'd hate to see anything happen to him, she thought, shuddering a bit despite the balminess of the June night. Unbidden, a vision of the anonymous "Mr. Smith" arose. She would be a long time forgetting his scowl as he stalked in fury out of the cabin. And then there was Buck Younger, perhaps. Someone else, certainly, who had displayed an undue amount of interest in the *Albatross*.

There had to be a reason — and an awfully

good one, too. Some very definite purpose lay behind the various attempts to gain title to the *Albatross.*

Something is on that houseboat! The words exploded from Jackie's subconscious. The longer she mulled over the idea, the more certain she became that this was the explanation. What else could account for the houseboat's vast popularity? But what could this "something" be? And what was it doing aboard the *Albatross?*

CHAPTER THREE

Saturday morning, Jackie and Val ate a quick breakfast before hurrying down the overgrown path through the woodland back of the house. A few minutes later, the *Albatross* churned into view.

As the girls waved from the shore, the houseboat's engines slowed for the tricky approach to the boulder-strewn inlet. Their waves turned to cheers when at last the barrier was crossed and the anchor dropped with a splash that sent water geysering high into the air.

The boys, dungaree-clad and barefoot, swaggered down the gangplank.

"Shouldn't someone tell the Matson Line about these nautical geniuses?" Val teased.

"Do you think they'd become commodores right away? Or would they have to settle for mere captaincies?" Jackie pretended to wonder.

Taking the razzing with good humor, the boys bent to the task of making the *Albatross* fast to shore.

"Did you get all your final papers without any trouble?" Jackie asked.

Whit nodded, but an angry look flickered briefly over his face. "No, nothing you'd call trouble, exactly," he said. "Just that Smith character hanging around again. He offered Mr. Dodson a whopping bribe to cancel our agreement. The old man threatened to call the police if he showed up at the dockyard again."

"Do you suppose there might be a reason why the *Albatross* is so popular?" Jackie asked carefully, apprehensive that she might be taunted about her wild imagination.

Whit shot her an appreciative look. "That occurred to you, too? My suspicions started to rise the minute Smith went for his wallet."

"We spent three hours last night searching that boat from prowl to keel," Greg said. "If there ever was a pirate treasure or something concealed aboard her, it isn't there now."

"In that case, we can just forget about Mr. Smith and all the other menacing rivals you three have conjured up," Val said firmly. "Pretty soon we won't have time to loaf around; we'll have to buckle down and start getting things in shape for the wedding."

"To think I've met my doom so young!" Greg moaned, but it was obvious that he wouldn't have traded one of Val's dimples for an admiral's stripes.

Val proposed a picnic, an idea which the others quickly seconded. They made a foray on the Prescott refrigerator, then returned to the beach to eat, talk, and swim the day away.

Late that afternoon, Whit boarded the *Albatross*, and presently he rejoined his companions carrying a dog-eared catalogue. Using the damp sand as a tablet, he estimated the cost of the furniture and equipment which would be needed to start the houseboat-restaurant in business.

"I hadn't figured on everything being so expensive," he said in a worried tone. He added that even at wholesale prices his budget could not possibly stretch enough to cover the cost of all the tables and chairs, as well as the enormous amount of dishes, flatware, and linen that would be needed.

"Why don't you buy some of the things second hand?" Jackie suggested. "We can all scout around for a cafe that's going out of business. In that way, you could buy what you need at half-price, or even less."

Whit solved a quick problem in long division.

"We could swing that," he agreed. "Buying the stuff at half-price would leave us enough capital to install a modern range and dishwasher, too."

"We'll look around first, and if we don't find anything suitable, perhaps an ad in the paper would smoke out a place," Jackie proposed.

Greg laughed. "I think it's all a plot to drum up business for the *Courier*!" Nevertheless, he agreed that her idea was sound.

Whit was anxious to have the refurbishment well under way by the time Roger Nelson, his partner, arrived. The young couples spent the rest of the afternoon pacing off the decks of the houseboat and computing the amount of paint, primer, cleanser and detergent required to give the *Albatross* the trim, spotless appearance which would attract customers.

Returning to the house at six o'clock, Jackie found a telephone message awaiting her.

"Melinda wants me to cover Terri Nicholson's deb dance!" she exclaimed with a mixture of excitement and regret, since Whit had already asked her out for the evening.

"Miss Foster said she didn't feel up to attending herself," Mrs. Prescott called from the kitchen. "I'm afraid it doesn't give you much notice. Can you be there by nine? She also mentioned that you were welcome to bring an escort."

"Would you like to come with me, Whit?" Jackie asked eagerly. "We could have just as much fun — Oh! It's black tie."

"You're in luck," he replied loftily. "The best men at weddings nowadays come fully equipped with black ties — and white dinner jackets. Pick you up at eight-thirty."

Jackie raced through a shampoo and shower. She borrowed Mrs. Prescott's hair dryer to set her curls, and gave herself a manicure. When the doorbell chimed, she was dabbing cologne to her wrists and temples.

"I'm coming!"

She spun once in front of the mirror, admiring the swirl of her lemon-yellow gown with its flared skirt, then draped a matching stole around her shoulders.

Whit's smile showed his very evident approval. After a complimentary remark about her appearance, he mentioned that Mr. Prescott had offered them the loan of his car.

Jackie decided that in his white dinner jacket and with his red crewcut freshly trimmed, Whit was the handsomest escort she had had in months. She was also secretly delighted that, even while wearing the highest pair of heels she possessed, the top of her head barely brushed his chin.

Most of the guests were already assembled when they arrived. Jackie whipped a pen and notebook from her purse as the debutante, radiant in bouffant white, made her grand entrance. For the next half hour, she concentrated on identifying half-forgotten faces, jotting down gown details, and filling page after page with notes regarding floral decorations and the superb buffet dinner of which the guests would partake later.

Pausing to relax her cramped fingers, Jackie looked around for Whit and caught sight of him cha-chaing with a raven-haired girl in a snug, strapless dress. The girl appeared to be listening breathlessly to his every word. And Whit seemed to be enjoying her adulation!

I have enough data to fill three articles, Jackie abruptly decided. She tucked the pen and notebook back in her evening bag, determined that there they could stay for the remainder of the evening. She wasn't jealous, of course, but —

To her relieved delight, Whit escorted his sophisticated partner back to her seat as soon as the dance ended, and shouldered his way through the crush of couples to Jackie's side.

"Have you ever," he asked with an amused grin, "been tickled under the chin by a pair of false eyelashes? It's quite an experience!"

Jackie shared his laughter, glad now that she had not attempted anything along the lines of heavy glamour herself. When the members of the orchestra bongoed their way into a rhumba, she at first insisted on dancing at arm's length, until Whit drew her closer.

"Just keeping my eyelashes out of harm's way," she explained demurely.

"Yours aren't phony!"

The midnight buffet tasted as delectable as it had looked, and after they had circled the floor in a final waltz and said their good nights to their hostess, Jackie exclaimed that she had never enjoyed a party so thoroughly.

"Care for a short stroll?" Whit suggested, cutting the motor after pulling up in front of the Prescotts' garage. "Only to help work off the anchovies," he added innocently, when she hesitated.

Jackie laughed and took his hand. Whit was fun and, so far, had proved himself to be definitely unwolfish. In an amiable silence, they sauntered up a knoll which commanded a view of the moonlit sea.

"Santa Teresa is a beautiful town," Whit said sincerely. "Exactly the spot I've always wanted to settle down in. I'm glad Greg talked me into coming here."

"So am I," Jackie admitted. "Val's wedding —" Suddenly she stopped, raising on tiptoe to peer over a clump of low-growing trees at the water's edge. "That's odd," she murmured. "I thought I saw a light down there."

Whit tensed. Dropping her hand, he strode forward a few paces.

"There it is again!" Jackie cried, pointing.

But Whit, too, had seen the pinpoint flash. "Let's go," he said, tight-lipped. "Somebody is on the *Albatross*!"

"Wait!" Jackie caught Whit's arm, restraining him from hurtling down the rocky slope. "You'd only break a leg going through there in the dark. Besides, it's quicker by car — there's an abandoned road just the other side of the grove."

Whit steadied her across the slick patches of grass as they raced toward the driveway. He had the motor turning over before she was half in the seat, and an instant later, they were rocketing down the quiet street.

"There!" Jackie indicated the turn.

Whit shifted into low gear, exclaiming in disgust at the ruts that snatched at the tires and pitched the car into the center of the road. Reluctantly, he eased up on the accelerator. "I've thought of a hundred questions to ask about that houseboat in the past twenty-four hours," he said grimly. "Now maybe we can get a few answers!"

Jackie felt certain that an urgent reason lay behind the interloper's nocturnal visit to the *Albatross*. She glanced anxiously at the determined young man beside her. "But — you

44

and Greg searched the boat, didn't you?"

"Sure," Whit affirmed. "That doesn't mean a thing. We didn't know where to look, or even what we were looking for. We didn't rip up the decks, pump out the gas tanks. To be positive of finding every secret cranny, we'd have to put the *Albatross* in drydock and take her apart nail by nail."

"It's hard to know what to think," Jackie murmured. They would, she decided hopefully, know a great deal more about the riddle of the *Albatross* if they were successful in surprising the intruder at his search.

She peered ahead at the swarm of insects trapped in the glow of the headlights, praying that the person aboard the houseboat was too much absorbed in his errand to pay attention to anything else.

As they neared the inlet, the road deteriorated into a web of ruts and chuckholes, so crisscrossed and deep that the brilliant beams of light jiggled crazily, illuminating bits of trees and shrubs and, now and then, a patch of black, swirling water. The powerful headlights would advertise their approach as effectively as a siren!

Whit seemed to read her thoughts. Cautiously, he pulled up on the pitted shoulder of the road and cut the ignition.

"I'm afraid of breaking an axle if we drive

any farther," he told her. "Feel up to a hike?"

"Nothing like a stroll in the country to work off the anchovies," Jackie returned. She hopped out, trying not to think what the brambles and stones would do to her sandals and nylons. "We haven't far to go, have we?"

"Just a few hundred yards." Whit pitched his voice low, aware that sounds carry a considerable distance over water.

Following the road's rugged curve, they hurried toward the mouth of the inlet. Within a few minutes, they were able to make out the dark shape of the *Albatross* rocking at anchor and to hear the lapping of waves across her keel.

"Do you think he's still —" Jackie started to ask, and then, not watching her footing, stumbled as her heel twisted on a rock. Whit caught her before she could pitch forward, but the rock skipped over the ledge formed by the gravel shoulder of the road and dislodged a nest of pebbles, which tumbled noisily into the sea.

"Oh!" Jackie bit her lip in disgust. The clamor had aroused swift activity aboard the houseboat. From across the water, she heard the echo of running feet, followed by a loud, hollow thud. Seconds later, a sputtering hiccough growled twice before resolving itself

46

into a steady putt-putt-putt fading toward the open sea.

Whit had sprinted ahead, but he was unable to catch more than a shadowy glimpse of the figure crouching in the motorboat.

"He's half a mile away by now," he said gloomily, striding back.

"I really put my foot into it that time," Jackie scolded herself. "Whit, I *am* sorry!"

"Forget it — we had about one chance in a thousand, anyway. The slightest noise would have alerted him. You notice he had that motorboat all primed for a quick getaway."

Clinging to Whit's arm, Jackie hobbled mournfully along. Even though he didn't blame her for the blunder, she could sense his deep disappointment. An answer to the mystery of the *Albatross* had been almost within his grasp — until she had kicked it out of his reach.

"Perhaps we frightened him away before he found whatever he came for." She offered the faint consolation hopefully.

Whit allowed her to precede him up the gangplank, which swayed creakingly in the night breeze, then strode across the deck. "I'm half-inclined to hope that he got it," he growled. "Maybe then we'd get a little peace and —" He bit off the sentence as, wrenching open the cabin door, his eyes fell

47

upon the wild disarray inside.

"Oh, what a mess!" Jackie gasped.

Whit snapped on the light powered by the boat's generator. Following him inside, Jackie saw that the bunks had been ripped apart and the heavy chairs upended. Books, papers, pictures were strewn about and tossed carelessly into corners. Even the light fixture had been unscrewed, leaving the bare bulb dangling glaringly from the ceiling.

"The next room is in even worse shape," Whit reported glumly, returning from a hasty inspection tour. "Looks as if he had just started on the galley — only a couple of cupboards disturbed there."

"That's a good sign," Jackie offered hopefully. "If he was still searching when we interrupted him, it means he didn't find what he was looking for. I imagine he was slowed down considerably by having to rely on a flashlight."

"Maybe we ought to hold open houseboat," Whit grumbled. "Burglars welcome Tuesdays and Thursdays."

He wrestled a chair upright and climbed on the seat to replace the light fixture. Jackie stooped to collect the scattered books and papers. "Are you going to notify the police?" she asked.

"I don't see what good it would do. Anyone

would know better than to leave his fingerprints lying around. And I'm afraid that if this got into the papers the unpleasant advance publicity might jinx our restaurant business."

"Yes, I can see that people might be wary of a place that is reputed to have the crown jewels or a pirate treasure stashed away in a sliding bulkhead," Jackie agreed. She stacked a handful of books on the shelf. "Whit, what do you suppose it *is*?"

"To me, it looks like a place that's just had a rodeo held in it," observed a wry voice behind them.

Jackie whirled to see Greg leaning against the door frame.

"You won't think it's so funny when you have to sleep on a mattress that's had half its stuffing gouged out," Whit predicted.

While he and Jackie sketched in the details of the prowler's discovery and escape, Greg rolled up his sleeves and helped them restore order to the cabin.

"I can't see that anything is missing," he said presently.

"Would we know if it was?" Whit countered.

"I don't believe the burglar was after anything you boys own," Jackie said. "I have an idea he thinks Lance Shelby concealed

49

something of value here."

"Lance Shelby!" Greg exclaimed. "Was this *his* houseboat?"

"Why, yes." Jackie eyed him curiously. "Did you know him?"

"He visited the base early this month," Greg said. "He had been granted permission to interview Admiral Billingsly. A lot of the brass sat in on the conference, and since I was acting as the admiral's aide at the time, I stayed during the interview. Saw quite a lot of Shelby."

"You'd have thought he was the President come to bestow a couple of light cruisers on the fleet, the way everyone catered to him," Whit contributed. He snapped his fingers. "Speaking of Lance Shelby, didn't Buck Younger trigger off that riot in front of the admiral's quarters the same evening the great newsman arrived?"

Greg nodded. "What a brawl! Took every Shore Patrolman in Port Dixon to break it up. I don't think anyone ever did discover what it was all about, but Buck was headed for a long stretch in the brig because of it."

"He broke out a couple of days later, though, and nobody's seen him since." Whit frowned suddenly. "And wasn't it the very next morning that they discovered —"

Jackie intercepted the warning look that

Greg shot his friend. "Discovered what?" she prompted.

"Me and my big mouth!" Whit groaned. "Sorry, Miss T. Military secret."

Jackie did not press him. For a moment, though, the conversational trend had reminded her of something, some obscure piece of information that she had recently garnered while reading or watching a news telecast. The vague memory skipped away before her brain could really take hold of it. She stifled a yawn, realizing that she was much too sleepy to think clearly. Probably, she told herself, it concerned something quite unimportant, anyway.

CHAPTER FOUR

Jackie slept late the next morning, awaking barely in time to shower and dress before attending church services. Although invited to come along, she had decided against accompanying Val to her aunt's home, where the entire Prescott family planned to gather for a relative's birthday party. Instead, she purchased a fat Sunday newspaper and carried it to a park bench.

"Houses, flats — here we are, apartments, furnished," she murmured, creasing open the want-ads section. Unless she found an apartment within the next three weeks she would have no choice but to give up her job and return to Los Angeles.

How disgusting! she fretted, when the tightly crammed columns revealed nothing suitable in a moderate price range. If only I had left work early last Friday. Just an hour sooner and I would have had first crack at that houseboat.

Then she was forced to smile. The situation

wasn't quite that desperate yet. And, she reminded herself, Whit intended to make very good use of the *Albatross*. In any case, she would have found it difficult to cope with the bewildering assortment of persons who continued to demonstrate their interest in the houseboat — even to the point of illegal entry.

"I'd like to know if that awful Mr. Smith was our burglar of last night," Jackie mused aloud.

She considered it quite likely that the stocky foreigner was the culprit. But then again, it might also have been the man with the Southern drawl.

"If Whit was right and the man he saw in the car *was* Buck Younger, what connection might *he* have with the *Albatross*?" she asked herself.

The mention of the brawling Texan reminded her of the abruptly terminated conversation of the night before. What sort of military secret could possibly have involved a rough-and-tumble sailor like Buck Younger? Again, she struggled to retrieve the dim memory that had teased her brain, but whatever it was had firmly entrenched itself in her subconscious, and no amount of puzzling could coax it out.

Well, anyway, I'll bet the mystery has something to do with Lance Shelby, Jackie thought, abandoning side issues like Buck Younger. Think of the secrets a famous newspaperman might uncover!

Perhaps Lance Shelby had obtained documents which incriminated a gang of racketeers. These criminals would certainly attempt to recover such evidence before the police learned of the newspaperman's discovery. But why such concentration on the houseboat? Why not search his desk at the *Courier* office — or his apartment?

How do I know they haven't? Jackie thought suddenly. With reporters and cameramen bustling in and out of the newspaper building at all hours of the day and night, it would be almost impossible for anyone to ransack his desk. To desperate men, though, Lance Shelby's apartment would be easily accessible.

She deposited the papers in the nearest trash can, at the same time trying to remember the address that Ted Rigney had mentioned. She had boarded a bus and was on her way downtown before she paused to wonder how she might gain entry to the ace reporter's penthouse.

I'm hunting for an apartment, and his is vacant. What better excuse do I need? she decided.

Despite the simplicity of her plan, Jackie

felt some trepidation as a uniformed doorman bowed her into a lavishly decorated foyer. Everything in the apartment building had an aura of wealth surrounding it. Everything, she amended, but herself. Supposing the manager refused to admit her?

"There's only one way to find out," she told herself. Taking a deep breath, she readied her sunniest smile and pressed the button beneath the card labeled "Superintendent."

Jackie heard the gong reverberate loudly behind the closed door, but no footsteps responded in answer to the summons. After a minute or two, she pressed the buzzer again. The bell had just echoed a second time when feet shuffled down the polished expanse of corridor and an elderly man in work clothes appeared.

"Mr. Post is gone. He'sa come back two or two-thirty," the old man said.

"Oh, dear, that's too bad." Jackie started to turn away, but the janitor's Italian accent had evoked a memory. "Why, Mr. Orsini!" she exclaimed, recognizing the former custodian of the high school. "How nice to see you again."

He smiled widely, pleased at being remembered. "You want to see Mr. Post?"

"Not really. I came to look at the vacant apartment," Jackie explained. "I'm working here in town now, and I need a place to live."

The janitor shook his head. "You don't need this one. It'sa too expensive. But come on. I show you." He drew a jingling ring of keys from his pocket and stepped into a self-service elevator.

"I understand the man who leased the apartment has recently died," Jackie said as the elevator ascended. "Are his things still here?"

Mr. Orsini nodded. "Maria, my wife, she clean the apartment Friday. Mr. Post say pretty soon relatives come, take everything away. Might as well have the place looking nice."

But, Jackie thought as the door swung open and she stepped onto the thick, rich pile of the carpet, Maria's work had all been in vain. The penthouse most decidedly did not look nice.

Behind her, Mr. Orsini gasped and began gesticulating frantically. "Somebody wreck everything!" he moaned, clapping his hands to his head. "Mr. Post will be plenty mad!"

Appalled as she was by the wanton destruction, Jackie felt no shock of surprise. She had almost expected to find the penthouse in a state of chaos similar to that which the midnight prowler had left behind on the *Albatross*.

Jackie was now convinced that it was the

sullen "Mr. Smith" who was responsible for the rifling of Lance Shelby's possessions, since the man with the Southern drawl had apparently not arrived in Santa Teresa until Friday evening. On Thursday morning, he had been in a phone booth in Port Dixon. By late the next afternoon, he had still not made an appearance at the dock, but had resorted to another telephone call in the hope of persuading Mr. Dodson to refrain from selling the *Albatross* until he arrived.

I wonder why it took him so long? she pondered. Greg and Whit made the drive from Port Dixon in a couple of hours. It seems to me if the Southerner wanted the houseboat so badly, he would have broken every traffic law in the book to get to it first.

"You don't want the apartment, eh?"

Jackie realized that Mr. Orsini was waiting for her to leave the elevator. "No, I don't think so," she said. "Thank you for showing the apartment to me, but I'm afraid it would cost a great deal more than I can afford."

"You be better off with a nice cheap place bandits don't break into," he said morosely, pausing at the superintendent's office.

Jackie left the building and resumed the train of thought he had interrupted. If Mr. Smith's motives were difficult to figure out, the Southerner was a real enigma. Unless —

Her eyes widened. Unless the Southerner was Buck Younger!

He wouldn't dare break any traffic laws, she thought. I'll bet he detoured miles out of his way every time he saw a policeman. With the Shore Patrol after him for desertion, he couldn't risk being recognized.

When Whit had first suggested that the Southern voice on the phone might have belonged to Buck Younger, Greg had argued that the Texan would have no reason to linger in California. Jackie could still think of no motive why he should do so, but nevertheless, she strongly believed that Whit's hunch had been correct. Buck Younger, as well as Mr. Smith, was interested in that houseboat — or in something that he suspected was concealed on it.

Jackie took a few more steps, then halted, oblivious to the curious stares she was drawing from her fellow pedestrians. "There might be a way to find out what the mysterious something is," she murmured. "If Lance Shelby was working on a hot story just before he flew to the Orient, someone at the *Courier* might know about it."

A brisk ten-minute walk brought her to the newspaper building. A cameraman, she decided, would have been Shelby's most likely confidant, since the reporter might have needed pictures to accompany his story. She rode up to the third floor, but found the photographic department deserted. Undaunted, she hiked up another flight of stairs. The photographers quite often spent time in the City Room when not working on a specific assignment.

To her disappointment, however, most of the rooms on this floor were also empty. Not until she reached her own department did she encounter anyone, and then it was Melinda Foster. The Society Editor sat pecking half-heartedly away at a batch of items for her column.

"Don't you ever take a day off?" Jackie asked her.

Melinda smiled wanly. "I prefer to keep busy. But what are you doing here on such a beautiful Sunday afternoon?"

"I was looking for one of the cameramen. They all seem to be out, though." Jackie sank into a chair beside the older girl's desk. "Melinda," she said impulsively, "you knew Lance Shelby pretty well, didn't you? Would you have any idea of what he was working on just before —"

Melinda swayed, gripping her typewriter with both hands. Every drop of color had drained out of her face, and her entire concentration was riveted on a spot ten feet away.

59

"What is it? What's wrong?" Jackie cried. Following Melinda's stupefied gaze, she, too, was impelled to turn.

A tall, dark, and very handsome man stood in the doorway. His arms were folded and a cigarette dangled rakishly between his lips.

"Just before what?" Lance Shelby demanded, advancing into the room.

For a minute longer, Jackie struggled to regain her composure. There were no ghosts, she told herself sternly, and spooks and spirits materialized only at seances under the adroit manipulation of phony fortune tellers.

Glancing anxiously at Melinda's waxen face, she hurried to the water cooler and returned to press the cup into the older girl's hand. The question she ignored. This was hardly the time to go on with a sentence that had almost ended in the words, "just before he died."

Because, incredible as it seemed, Lance Shelby was very much alive.

The reporter appeared to be genuinely bewildered.

"Well, come on. Isn't anyone even going to say hello?" he expostulated. "You two characters act as if you'd seen a gho— Oh, ho! Everything has suddenly become very clear."

Wheeling abruptly, he strode to the oak-paneled partition at the opposite end of the room. He shoved through Bruce Mac-Farland's private door and rummaged through the editor's desk. With the gusto of an infant tornado, he came breezing back, flapping a beige-colored envelope against the palm of his hand.

"Doesn't anyone ever read his mail around here?" he exclaimed aggrievedly. "I sent this message from the Honolulu airport nearly ten hours ago!"

"Lance, we thought you were dead." Melinda had regained her voice. "That plane crashed!"

He nodded. "So I hear. Lucky for me, I wasn't aboard."

"You must have known that everyone here would be frantic with worry." Jackie's sharp tone held none of the deference usually accorded the star reporter. "Why didn't you cable or telephone as soon as you learned what had happened?"

"Now hold everything! I hadn't the foggiest notion until early this morning that my name was listed among the missing. Believe me, it was a greater shock to me than it was to you!"

Lance slung a leg over the corner of Melinda's desk, treating the girls to one of his famous, off-center smiles.

"Through no fault of my own, I was detained in Hong Kong. The plane on which

I held reservations took off without me. Apparently, nobody bothered to cross my name off the passenger manifest, since everyone seems to have taken it for granted that I was aboard." He shrugged. "When I'm busy chasing down a lead, I don't go browsing through every newssheet published in the Far East. I knew nothing of the exaggerated reports of my demise until I landed in Honolulu this morning. Dashed off a cable right away then, of course, but —"

"Oh, what does it matter now?" Melinda cried happily. "You're safe; that's all that counts!"

"My opinion exactly." Lance flicked his hat to the back of his head. "Guess our esteemed editor will be glad to see me back, too. Don't know what he'd use for copy if I weren't around."

Jackie gasped. What overbearing egotism! Granted, Lance Shelby had plenty to be conceited about. He was talented — and handsome — and charming. But she could not help feeling that all of these attributes could be enhanced by at least a semblance of modesty.

His personality flaws were none of her business, though, Jackie told herself. She opened her purse and fished for the notebook she had used the night before.

"See you in the morning," she said, dropping it into her desk drawer. "I really just stopped by to leave my notes on the Nicholson dance."

Melinda smiled absent-mindedly. Before Jackie could reach the hall, however, Lance Shelby's voice arrested her.

"Sure that was your only reason for paying a Sunday call on the *Courier?* Somehow I got the impression that you were digging for information about me." He tilted a sardonic eyebrow. "Research for my obituary?"

Jackie had been hoping to escape before the subject of her unfinished query recurred to him. Certainly she had no desire to break the news that the mistaken announcement of his death had prompted sight-seers to route a series of excursions through his belongings.

"I'm afraid the only obituaries I write concern parties that die on the vine," she hedged.

"Then why ask what story I had been working on?" he persisted reasonably.

There seemed no way to avoid replying. Jackie took a deep breath. "If you must know, the man who bought the houseboat you used to rent is a friend of mine. I thought that if you had been investigating the activities of gangsters or racketeers, it might account for some of the strange things that have been happening aboard the *Albatross.*"

"*Bought* the houseboat!" Lance Shelby roared, leaping to his feet.

"Like everyone else, Mr. Dodson thought you were on the plane that crashed," Jackie explained. "Since you only rented the boat by the month, he put the *Albatross* up for sale."

"Goodness, Lance, it's not that important," Melinda declared. "I never could understand why you kept that creaky old boat, anyway."

"I happen," he said, "to be very fond of fishing."

"All your gear is in a storage room at Dodson's," Jackie put in helpfully.

This statement seemed to relieve his mind. "Just so long as he didn't include my tackle in the sale, I guess it's all right," he conceded. "Uh — you mentioned that strange things have been happening?"

Lance Shelby's attitude had undergone a quick change. Now he was all news-scenting reporter.

"Yes," Jackie said, deciding that her snap judgment of him might have been faulty. "Several people were interested in the *Albatross*, but my friend succeeded in buying it first. Both he and Mr. Dodson were offered bribes to cancel the sale, and when they refused, an attempt was made last night to rob the boat."

"Is your friend wealthy?" asked Melinda.

Jackie smiled. "No, quite the contrary. Nothing of his was taken. So we assumed that since Whit had nothing of value there, the thief must have been hunting for something belonging to the houseboat's former owner. Did you keep anything expensive aboard the *Albatross*, Mr. Shelby?"

"My fishing tackle wasn't cheap," he admitted. "By the way, everyone calls me Lance. Now, what was that about my investigating racketeers and gangsters?"

"A number of your articles have concerned notorious criminals. As there seemed to be no other explanation for the houseboat's popularity, I thought you might have come across some incriminating evidence concerning underworld life."

"And cached the evidence aboard my floating oyster palace?" Lance grinned. "Quite an idea. Wish I had thought of it myself."

"Then you don't know of anything concealed on the *Albatross*?" Jackie bit her lip, chagrined. So much for her elaborate theories!

"Nothing except your friend — Whit, is it?" Lance slid off the desk where he had been perched. "I wonder if he'd mind my taking a quick look around the old tub just to make

65

sure the Dodsons didn't overlook any of my gear. Some of those lures would be hard to replace."

"Of course he wouldn't mind. I had intended to drop by there this afternoon, if you'd care to come along."

"Hey, what about me?" Melinda cried.

Lance gave her a friendly but definitely non-romantic pat on the shoulder. "Honey, I'm a working reporter, remember? And I've got a hunch there's a hot story lurking around here somewhere!"

His sleek Italian sports car was parked at the curb in open defiance of the "tow-away zone" sign posted above it. Ducking low to enter the car, Jackie shook her head in wonderment. Lance Shelby, she mused, seemed to be one of fortune's favorites. Beautiful girls like Melinda Foster idolized him, fabulous trips to the Orient were a routine part of his life, and traffic cops handed out their citations on the next street down. No wonder the *Courier*'s star reporter was a wee bit conceited!

She gave directions as he skillfully guided the car around corners and down grades. Presently she found herself responding to questions about herself and her friends. Lance's manner was so friendly that, without hesitation, she detailed Whit's experiences in purchasing the houseboat, and mentioned his difficulties with the recalcitrant "Mr. Smith."

"You think he was using an alias?" Lance probed. "Could be I've run across this 'Mr. Smith.' Give me his description."

Jackie had no trouble in complying; the man had left an indelible impression on her mind. "A stocky man in his mid-forties, about five feet nine, with black eyes and haystack eyebrows," she told Shelby. "He needed a haircut and his suit was rumpled."

A thoughtful expression crossed Lance's face, but "dunno for sure" was the only reply she managed to drag from him when she asked if he could identify the man.

Pulling off the rutted road at approximately the same spot where Whit had parked the evening before, Lance shaded his eyes and peered toward the inlet. "Looks as if your friend has company already." He gestured to the motor launch that nuzzled the bow of the *Albatross*.

Jackie was forced to take rapid strides in order to keep up with the reporter. As they drew closer to the little bay, she perceived the reason for his haste. The visiting craft bore the Coast Guard insignia, and Lance, already intrigued by her accounts of the mystery surrounding the *Albatross*, intended to discover the purpose behind this official call.

Ascending the gangplank, Jackie found

Whit and Greg deeply absorbed in conversation with a pair of Naval policemen. Each of the men wore S.P. armbands, and around the waists of their white uniforms were buckled businesslike service revolvers.

"Has something else happened?" she asked Whit, who broke away from the group and came to greet her.

"Not to us. To Buck Younger, if and when they catch him." He looked quizzically at Lance Shelby, and Jackie introduced him.

"Lance Shelby!" Whit exclaimed. "But aren't you —?"

"Still among the living." Lance smiled, and briefly explained.

"Sorry. That was thoughtless of me," Whit apologized. He swung back to Jackie. "Remember the other evening I thought I saw Buck Younger cruise past the wharf? Seems I was right, after all. The city police had set up a roadblock that night trying to nab a bank robber, and one of the cars they admitted through was driven by Buck. The patrolman checked his license as a matter of routine, but he didn't realize until later that Younger was the man the Navy had a warrant out on."

This confirmed Jackie's theory regarding the telephone caller with the Southern accent. Deciding to save this news until later, she asked, "What are the Shore Patrolmen doing here?"

"They're running a check on all Naval personnel and recent dischargees in the area. They're hoping that someone who knew Buck personally might be able to give them a lead as to his present whereabouts."

Whit took her arm and drew her into the group. Lance tagged behind. Jackie, masking a smile, reflected that the lucky newspaperman had stumbled onto the makings of another "scoop." Talk about fortune's favorites!

"We have no idea what he could be doing in this locality," one of the Shore Patrolmen was saying to Greg. "Unless he has made contact with the person who helped him crash out of the brig."

"You mean the escape wasn't his own doing?" Greg asked, startled.

"Definitely not. The guard was attacked from behind and his keys stolen. Younger was the only prisoner in custody at the time, so we have no witnesses who saw the break-out." The Naval policeman fingered his belt. "Funny thing. Younger got into a lot of scrapes during his years with the Navy, but in each case, he operated as a lone wolf. Always by himself. Seems odd that anyone would be willing to take such a risk for him now."

"Yes, it does," Whit agreed, escorting the patrolmen to the gangplank. "If we see or hear anything, we'll let you know right away."

The launch roared out of the inlet, heading back toward the public docks of Santa Teresa.

Jackie was struck by the thoughtful expression that had settled over Greg's face at the mention of Younger's accomplice. He made no mention of the A.W.O.L. Texan, however, but extended his hand to Lance Shelby.

"Nice to see you again, sir," he said politely. "We enjoyed reading your piece on Admiral Billingsly."

"Had a ball doing it," Lance replied. "The fishing is good down around Port Dixon. I just tossed the anchor over the side and set my lines while banging out the article. Had a half-dozen bass by the time I finished typing up the interview."

"They ought to change that 'Life of Riley' saying to read 'Life of Shelby,' " Whit observed. "I, uh, I feel a bit guilty having bought the *Albatross* out from under you. Of course I had no idea —"

"Of course not," Lance interjected smoothly. "Even my editor was prepared to write me off with a floral R.I.P." His casual glance traveled the length of the houseboat. "You haven't run across any of my tackle,

70

have you? I haven't been down to check it out at Dodson's yet, but it was scattered all over the boat. He might have missed packing a rod or a few lures."

"Haven't seen so much as a fishhook, but you're welcome to look for yourself," Whit offered. Like a proper host, he opened a cabin door and escorted the reporter inside. Within a few minutes, they emerged, empty-handed.

"Stay for a Coke?" Whit invited, but Lance declined.

"I'd better run back into town and play spook for a few people who haven't yet heard of my resurrection. Maybe I can scare Bruce MacFarland into giving me a raise. So long!"

CHAPTER FIVE

Greg, who had remained slouched in one of the canvas chairs while Whit accompanied Lance through the cabins, got to his feet and walked over to the railing. He remained there, lost in thought, until the reporter had vanished around the bend of the road.

"I wonder what's on his mind?" Jackie asked herself. "He has been acting awfully peculiar for the last half hour."

With a start, Greg aroused himself from the brown study into which he had sunk. "How long was Buck Younger in the brig before he crashed out?" he asked abruptly.

"Oh, two or three days, I suppose," Whit said, frowning. "Why?"

"Well, I was thinking —" Greg seemed to be having a mental debate with himself. "No, it couldn't be," he muttered. "Timing's all wrong."

Whit snapped his fingers in front of Greg's face, like a magician bringing his subject out of a trance. "It's me, remember, your old buddy, Greg. What are you stewing about?"

"My bomb of an idea turned out to be a dud." Greg stared glumly down at the frothing water. Suddenly, the glum look changed to one of startled comprehension. "Wait a minute!" he exclaimed. "I had it all backwards. The other guy wasn't the accomplice — Buck was!"

He wheeled around, and the cogs clicking in his brain were almost audible. "You're the one who put the notion into my head. You know — last night, when we were talking about the riot Buck started. You asked if it wasn't the very next day they discovered that the plans for that new atomic sub had been stolen —"

"No, pal," Whit said emphatically. "That's what I *started* to say. You shot me a dagger look and I shut up."

"Like a clam. You said, 'Sorry, Miss T. Military secret,' " Jackie verified. "But it isn't, really. It was in all the papers. About the plans having disappeared, I mean." And that, she remembered triumphantly, was exactly what she had been trying to recall. She had even clipped the item from the papers while comparing the different styles of the *Courier* and *Herald*!

Greg grimaced. "With friends like our newspapers, this country doesn't need ene-

73

mies," he growled. "That information shouldn't have been released."

"Have to keep the American public informed." Whit shrugged. "At least by releasing the news themselves, the authorities could play down its importance. Suppose a sharp newshound like Shelby had sniffed it out? He'd have blared it in three-inch headlines and had every Congressman in the country forming investigating committees to plague the Navy."

"Quit locking the sub door after the plans have been stolen and tell us your idea," Jackie said impatiently. "What about Buck Younger and his accomplice?"

The anger faded from Greg's face. "Usually visitors to Port Dixon are kept to a minimum and allowed in only on special passes. But two weeks ago when Shelby came to interview Admiral Billingsly, a crew of newsreel photographers sat in on the session, and half a dozen consulting engineers who had helped blueprint the new sub were there, too, surveying the harbor facilities. The base was bulging with visitors."

"I remember. All we needed was a drum and bugle corps to make it look like convention time at Madison Square Garden," Whit agreed. "Well, go on — get to the point."

"The point," said Greg earnestly, "is that

any one of those people, or even someone who slipped in with them during all the confusion, could have stolen the plans. But he couldn't just stroll in and pick them off the admiral's desk. They were in a locked steel cabinet, and a guard was posted in that office day and night. That's where I think Buck Younger came in."

"That big bruiser is too clumsy to be a safecracker," Whit protested. "The only thing he really knows how to do is fight."

"Exactly! As I said, the thief couldn't just walk into the admiral's office. He needed a diversion to pull the guard out of there first. My guess is that he hired Younger to start such a lulu of a brawl that every Shore Patrolman on the base would come running to squelch it. The Navy couldn't afford to let that mob of newsmen and photographers get wind of a riot — not with the Senate already bickering over military appropriations. So, while everyone else was pitching in to stop the battle, the thief jimmied the cabinet and did a Houdini act with the blueprints."

Whit was awed by his friend's deductive abilities. "Good lord, Greg, I think you've hit it!"

"It could easily have happened that way. And listen!" Jackie cried excitedly. "Buck Younger was the only one who could point

75

out the thief. He couldn't be allowed to come up before a court-martial — he might have confessed the whole scheme! So the thief slipped back onto the base a couple of nights later and sprung him out of the brig!"

"Stone walls do not a prison make, nor iron bars a cage — when you've got a friend on the outside," Whit added to an ancient poem.

"What was that you were saying before, about the timing being all wrong, Greg?" Jackie asked.

"Well, first I had the notion that Younger himself was the thief. He couldn't have been, though, because the guard didn't leave the admiral's office until *after* the fight had started. Buck was right in the thick of it the whole time. You know," he ruminated, "in some ways Port Dixon is a little like Alcatraz was. It's almost impossible to get in or out without a written pass. And when you do enter or leave, you're subjected to a search."

"So how did this mastermind get the blueprints past the gate?" Whit asked.

Greg casually exploded a bombshell. "He didn't. At least, I don't think so."

"They're still on the base?" Jackie gasped.

"Nope. I don't know where they are now," Greg admitted, "but I have a hunch that at one time they were right here on the *Albatross.*"

76

"Right here on the *Albatross*?" Whit echoed.

"You're not serious!" Jackie exclaimed.

But Greg was grimly earnest.

"Sure. It hit me a few minutes ago when Shelby mentioned that he had brought his houseboat down to Port Dixon. You know the setup there, Whit. A pass could be faked; an unauthorized person might get onto the base — and off again — but not with those blueprints. The guards at the gate use an X-ray type machine which would show up bulky papers, as well as any metal object. And if anyone had tried going over that twelve-foot electric fence, or taking off in a plane or 'copter, he'd have been spotted within seconds."

"Which leaves the water," Whit said, beginning to understand.

"That's the only way those papers *could* have been smuggled out." Greg paced a few yards down the deck, a faraway look in his eyes. "Shelby requested permission to bring his houseboat into the harbor while doing that interview. Because he is such a well-known person, authorization was granted almost immediately. Between then and the time he actually made the trip, any number of people might have learned of his plan. Shelby made no secret of the fact that he was an avid fisherman. He probably went around bragging

77

that he was going to get the interview and a good catch of fish in the bargain."

"I guess he bragged to one person too many," Jackie said with a little shiver.

"As I see it, the thief learned of Shelby's plans in advance, which gave him a chance to work out a timetable with Buck Younger. When the riot started and the guard ran out to help break it up, the thief slipped into the office and broke open the cabinet. Then he barreled down to where the *Albatross* was berthed, hid the plans aboard, and hurried back to rejoin his group. The whole operation shouldn't have taken more than half an hour."

"And with the blueprints safely concealed, he had no further need for haste." Whit took up the sordid tale. "He left when everyone else did, passed the gate search like any innocent citizen, and settled down in Santa Teresa to wait for Lance Shelby to return from his fishing trip. As soon as Shelby came ashore, the thief retrieved the cache." Whit brought his fist smashing down on the rail. "It was so simple it had to be foolproof. He couldn't miss!"

"Don't you think," Jackie interrupted quietly, "that 'thief' is the wrong word to use? Wouldn't 'spy' be more appropriate?"

"Well, let's just say that ordinary second-story men are more interested in diamond necklaces than in the blueprints for a nuclear sub," Greg admitted.

An uncomfortable silence settled over the *Albatross* as each of them was lost in his own thoughts. Jackie retraced the steps of Greg's reasoning and could find no flaw in it. The only trouble, she decided morosely, was that they hadn't figured out the ruse in time. The spy had neatly outfoxed them.

"Even that creepy Mr. Smith caught on before we did," she murmured to herself. "I wonder where he got the notion that the blueprints were still aboard the houseboat? Maybe he suspected that the spy hadn't been able to smuggle them out of the country yet, and figured this was as safe a temporary hiding place as any."

"I'll bet Buck Younger started worrying that he wasn't going to get his cut of the profits," Whit said, showing that his thoughts were running parallel to hers. "He took an awful risk coming out of hiding."

Greg nodded gloomily. He seemed to be blaming himself for not unraveling the plot sooner.

"What are you going to do now?" Jackie asked. "Notify the military authorities or the FBI?"

"Guess we'd better. Though, as you so

aptly put it, starting an investigation now is like locking the sub door after the plans have been stolen." Greg kicked absently at a splinter jutting up from the deck. "I want to think about it a little longer. I've got a feeling that somewhere along the way I overlooked an important point."

When Jackie left the houseboat a short time later, Whit and Greg had still not decided upon a definite course of action. Short-cutting along the woodland trail, she decided that the grandeur of the sunset in the western sky was out of place. A damp, murky fog would have made a more appropriate setting for her depressed frame of mind.

Her spirits sank even lower when she found the house empty and recalled the birthday party which the Prescott family was attending. It would be hours before Val and her parents would return.

Even now, Jackie could scarcely credit the fantastic tale which Greg had unfolded. Espionage in this peaceful little town!

The sharp jangle of the telephone bell sliced through her disturbed thoughts. Her eyes widened in surprise as Lance Shelby's breezy voice came bouncing over the wire.

"Hungry?" he asked without preamble.

"I had forgotten all about dinner," Jackie confessed.

"Then you're in luck. Slip into something black and slinky, and I'll buy you a lobster at Pietro's. Half an hour."

An uncompromising click severed the connection before Jackie could accept or reject the invitation. "Of all the nerve!" she fumed. "And telling me what to wear. It's a wonder he didn't specify the shade of lipstick —"

Suddenly she was overcome by a fit of giggles. It would do the conceited Mr. Shelby no end of good to be left waiting on the porch while she slipped out the back door. On the other hand, her stomach impatiently reminded her, she had eaten nothing since breakfast, and Pietro's was the best restaurant in town.

"Might as well attend the command performance," she told herself, still smiling as she hurried upstairs. Anything was preferable to sitting alone in an empty house and worrying about spies!

Jackie ignored his clothing instructions and chose a becoming knit suit in a soft shade of coral.

This mutinous gesture did nothing to diminish Lance's enthusiasm, however.

"My, my! You should be decorating the Society pages, instead of helping write them," he commented gallantly, holding the car door open for her.

Pietro's was hushed and dimly candlelit. A

bowing major domo whisked them to their table, where self-effacing waiters competed for the privilege of drawing out their chairs.

Goodness, thought Jackie, impressed by the service which Lance's very presence seemed to command. He certainly has the world handed to him on a platter. I'll bet he was born wearing twenty-four-carat diaper pins!

"I have a craving for seafood," Lance confided when the waiter had placed rosy goblets of shrimp cocktail before them. "That old 'brain food' legend was thrown at me when I was a kid. I had an urge to become the smartest fellow on the block, so fish was on the menu as often as I could persuade my folks to put it there. Guess I never outgrew the habit."

Jackie tasted the tiny crescents of shrimp nestling in a tangy sauce. "Um, this is wonderful," she exclaimed. "I can understand now why you're such a fishing fan."

"It's a wonderful hobby. I've had lots of relaxing vacations aboard that old houseboat. By the way," he asked, "what do your friends intend to do with the *Albatross*, now that they've bought her?"

"It's Whit's boat, really. Greg is just staying there with him for a few weeks. Whit plans to turn it into a restaurant."

Lance approved wholeheartedly. "Fine idea. It's a wonder no one thought of doing something like that sooner. I was rather surprised when the other young man — Greg — remembered me," he confided after a slight pause. "There were a great many visitors at Port Dixon the day I went down."

"Greg has a marvelous memory." Jackie smiled. "I think he must have had a 'brain food' diet, too."

It was on the tip of her tongue to reveal the brilliant way in which Greg had plotted the circumstances surrounding the theft of the blueprints. Just in time, she restrained the impulse. The slightest hint to a newsman of Lance's capabilities would have him burrowing for details. And the last thing Greg or the Navy wanted right now was more publicity!

"Besides," she substituted hastily, "why shouldn't he remember you? You're one of the best-known reporters on the West Coast. How about sharing the secret of your success and telling me how you reached such lofty heights?"

Lance considered. "Persistence. Determination. Luck, once in a while. My family had practically no money. I resolved to make up for it — be the richest kid on the block, as well as the smartest. You have to be tops if you want to get rich in the newspaper business. After working hours were over, I used to go out and make contacts. Pretty soon I had friends and informants in every walk of life, and leads to the big stories started trickling in. I made them pay off."

Jackie nodded, thinking that this driving determination explained a great deal about Lance Shelby. Vanity accounted for only a small part of his personality. A heaping portion of ruthlessness also figured in his outlook on life. Where his goals were concerned, nothing had been allowed to stand in the way.

"Well, you accomplished your aim," she conceded. "I doubt if many of the other kids on your block drive around in Italian sports cars, or fly to the Orient on routine assignments."

Lance disposed of the last succulent morsel of lobster. "My assignments are never routine," he corrected.

"Allow me to rephrase my statement," said Jackie humbly. "Lance Shelby flies to the Orient only on the most unique assignments. All right?" She smiled, and set down her coffee cup. "Tell me about Hong Kong."

Lance gave a sophisticated shrug. "It's very Chinese, nowadays."

A flurry of activity at a nearby table captured their attention. Someone's wineglass had overturned, and a waiter moved quickly to blot up the red stain which snaked across the snowy linen cloth.

Jackie's first glance at the scene of the mishap had been casual; her second was frankly incredulous. "Lance," she whispered, "the man at the corner table — he's the Mr. Smith I was telling you about!"

In a natural manner, as if merely wishing to summon the waiter, Lance swiveled. "Smith, nothing!" he said gleefully. "That's Alexei Litvinov!"

While Jackie was puzzling over this unrevealing piece of information, Lance rose unobtrusively and made his way to a phone booth.

"I've had the goods on Alexei for months, but he's always managed to elude me," the reporter said, returning by a route which kept his back to the unsuspecting foreigner.

"But — who is he?" Jackie whispered eagerly.

"Read the *Courier* tomorrow morning and find out," Lance teased. Amused by her crest-fallen expression, he relented. "Comrade Litvinov," he informed her *sotto voce*, "is one of those men who are popularly known on television dramas as espionage agents. Uncle Sam knows all about the little games he plays. The State Department refused him a visa when he applied for entry to this country last year."

"Then how did he get in? What's he doing here? And how," Jackie asked, "did you come to know him?"

"You sound like a pal of mine who hosts TV talk shows. Never lets the interviewee get a word in edgewise," Lance chided. "We don't have an iron curtain around America. Anyone with a reasonable amount of determination and intelligence can evade the border patrol and slip in illegally. I ran across Litvinov in Paris a couple of years back. At that time, he was a strike agitator — he and men like him stirred up all sorts of trouble for the French. They promoted a strike which literally crippled the country's transportation for six weeks."

Jackie's eyes widened. "Is that his mission in the United States?"

"My dear child," Lance said patronizingly, "Comrade Litvinov is a very versatile fellow. Not too many years ago he spied for the Soviets. Next he did a few jobs for the PLO. Lately there have been rumors about his ties to Saddam Hussein. . . . One never knows from day to day what dirty work he'll stick his pudgy little finger into next." He paused. "I can tell you this, though — I have a file in my safe-deposit box which contains a picture of him. It was snapped in a place which not even loyal American citizens are allowed to enter — unless the highly specialized nature of their work takes them there."

Jackie's mind was a whirl of names. Los Alamos, Oak Ridge, Cape Kennedy — that was the sort of place Lance meant!

"We'd better be going," he said, fanning bills across the discreetly reversed check on the platter. "I have a feeling that Pietro's is about to be invaded by the minions of the law!"

CHAPTER SIX

Spy! Spy! Spy! The word traveled through the *Courier* building with the rapidity of a brush fire leaping across the prairie. Everyone whom Jackie encountered that Monday morning was carrying a copy of the early edition. Her own paper was already dog-eared from having been read and reread.

"Iraqi Agent Apprehended!" the banner shrieked: and under Lance Shelby's by-line the story was dramatically revealed. The city police, acting on a tip from "your reporter," had placed Alexei Litvinov under arrest. An alerted FBI had already taken over custody of the suspected spy, and it was intimated that charges of espionage would be leveled against him. Definite proof of Litvinov's illicit activities, Lance wrote, had been placed in the hands of the Federal authorities.

Although the nature of the proof was not described, Jackie guessed that this must pertain to the compromising photograph in Lance's possession.

He certainly left no doubt in anyone's mind as to whom should be credited with the arrest, she thought with a mixture of amusement and annoyance.

References to "your reporter" were sprinkled liberally throughout the article. Even though it was Jackie who had been instrumental in the agent's identification, no mention was made of her participation. Actually, she felt rather relieved that her name had not appeared in the newspaper account. Melinda regarded Lance as her own special property — and Whit might not have understood, either.

"I wonder why he asked me out?" Jackie mused. "Maybe he is fascinated by new faces."

If so, she told herself ruefully, the fascination had soon worn off. Lance had barely spared the time to drive her home before returning to Pietro's to witness the capture of the secret agent. Examining her own feelings toward the *Courier*'s star reporter, she found that she could not decide whether she liked him or not.

I do and I don't, she thought, wrinkling her nose.

In any event, the date had supplied the answer to a point which Jackie had found perplexing. Greg's theory that the blueprints were at one time secreted aboard the *Albatross* explained why the houseboat was being searched. But Lance Shelby's apartment had also been ransacked. Now she realized that while Alexei Litvinov would have given a great deal to gain possession of the blueprints, his primary concern undoubtedly was to unearth the telltale photograph. No wonder "Mr. Smith" had gone to such desperate lengths in his attempts to buy the *Albatross*!

Melinda's pointed comment about the unopened mail brought her sharply back to earth. What a relief, Jackie thought, reaching for the letter opener, to have all the riddles solved. Well — all but one. There was still no clue as to the person who had purloined the vital documents. But that was a matter for the FBI. Now maybe Whit could redecorate his houseboat in peace — and she could concentrate on her job!

A few days later, the preparations for the wedding began in earnest. Lengthy consultations with florists, caterers, and photographers went on from morning till night, and strains of the *Wedding March* and *O Promise Me* echoed continuously from behind the door of the sunroom, where Val's Aunt Louise had taken over temporary possession of the piano.

"Do you realize," Val gasped, bursting into Jackie's bedroom on Thursday evening, "that we haven't even selected the bridesmaids' gowns yet? I put it off because Fran Harris left on vacation just before you arrived, and it went completely out of my mind!"

"That's not much of a problem," Jackie said. "Tobin's is having a sale. Now that the June brides are all married off, we can get the dresses for half-price. You're right, though," she admitted with a laugh when Val groaned despairingly. "We really ought to see about them. Since the wedding is only two weeks away, I suppose we'd better not wait for the quarter-price sale."

Val plopped down on the bed. "Jackie, how can you joke at a time like this?"

"It's easy — I'm not the bride-to-be!" Jackie had been sewing buttons onto a sweater. Now she set aside her needle and looked questioningly at her friend.

"You've been awfully nervous lately, Val," she said. "Is it just those famous pre-matrimonial jitters, or is something else the matter? I'd like to help if I can."

Val laughed shakily. "You're imagining things," she insisted. Then her composure crumpled. "Or maybe I am. It's Greg. He — he's seemed so withdrawn and preoccupied these past few days. He can be sitting right in the same room with me, and his mind is a million miles away."

"Oh, I see." Jackie stared reflectively out her bedroom window. The inlet was masked by close-growing trees, and the twilight effectively camouflaged any lights which might have twinkled aboard the *Albatross.*

"You mustn't worry," she said gently. "I think Greg is troubled about something that happened in Port Dixon shortly before his discharge. I heard him discussing it with Whit."

Val looked enormously relieved. "I'm glad to hear that. I was afraid he was trying to think of a diplomatic way to call off the wedding!" Curiously, she added, "What *did* happen in Port Dixon?"

"The blueprints for a new atomic submarine were stolen. There is a possibility that the man who was arrested the other night might have had something to do with the theft."

"Spies!" Val shuddered distastefully. "Thank goodness the FBI knows how to deal with people like that. Now," she reverted to her original concern, "what are we going to do about those dresses?"

"The stores are open tomorrow night. Why don't you and Fran meet me downtown after work?" Jackie suggested.

The next afternoon at five o'clock, the three

girls met outside the *Courier* building. Strolling along arm in arm, Jackie swapped news with Fran Harris, the pert redhead who was to be Val's other bridal attendant. They had all gone through school together, and since Jackie and Fran had not seen each other in two years, they found a great deal to talk about.

Luckily, Tobin's had a wide selection of bridesmaid's gowns left in stock. The girls had some difficulty in deciding which style and color they preferred, but finally they narrowed down the choice to a jacketed gown of mist-green taffeta and a lovely flaring chiffon in a heavenly shade of peacock blue.

"I believe the blue number suits both of you better." The saleswoman voiced her experienced opinion. "And aren't you fortunate to need no alterations? I wish I were a perfect size twelve."

After another quarter hour of twisting and turning before the full-length mirror, Jackie and Fran agreed that the saleswoman's advice was sound. They had the blue dresses carefully wrapped in layers of tissue paper and then, to complete the ensembles, they chose simple satin pumps and wide picture hats in a matching shade.

I wonder how Whit will like me in it, Jackie thought, juggling her parcels. A flush warmed her cheeks as she realized how very much she was looking forward to walking down the aisle as his partner after the marriage ceremony.

The past week had been so crowded that she had seen very little of the good looking ex-sailor. Social affairs seemed to be at a peak despite the fact that July was the height of the vacation season, and she and Melinda were often pressed for time to cover all the events to which they were invited. During her lunch hour, Jackie never failed to comb the want ads in the hope that a suitable apartment for rent would appear. She had even inserted an ad of her own in the *Courier*, but so far she had not received a single reply.

Something had better turn up soon, she thought. With the ceaseless comings and goings of caterers and photographers, it was beginning to seem as if she would never find another moment of solitude.

Whit, she knew, had been busy, too. A huge mound of paint and cleaning supplies now crowded the *Albatross'* center cabin, and Greg reported that considerable progress had already been made in the houseboat's refurbishment.

When Val mentioned that Greg planned to meet her downtown for dinner, Jackie glanced at her wristwatch. It was barely six o'clock. Several hours of daylight remained.

Impulsively, she decided to stop by the houseboat on her way home, and detoured around to the wrapping desk to request that her purchases be delivered.

"Have to rush — got a date. But I want to talk to you about something," Fran whispered as Val left the shop ahead of them. "Call you tomorrow."

Wondering what could be on Fran's mind, Jackie rode to the bus stop nearest the Prescott home and then walked the remaining distance to the inlet. She found Whit on his hands and knees, industriously running an electric sander over the deck. He seemed glad of an excuse to stop working.

"You've accomplished wonders this past week," Jackie praised him, looking around. "With a couple of days' vacation coming up, I thought I'd drop in to ask if you could use a helper."

Some of the weariness left his face and his eyes brightened. "I'll sign you on the ship's complement as soon as my fingers straighten out," he said gratefully. "What's your rating — able seaman, oiler, wiper?"

"Hummm. None of those categories quite describe my talents," Jackie said. "What does the bosun do?"

"Gives orders," said Whit, and laughed at her prompt "That's for me!"

Over a strawberry waffle and coffee, they discussed the next step in the houseboat's face-lifting.

"I have a few more yards of paint to finish chipping and then we can go ahead and prime," he told her proudly.

"I'll help," Jackie offered. She carried the dishes to the sink and paused thoughtfully, watching the soap bubble up around them.

"Whit," she said, "Val is worried about Greg. Do you know if he is still brooding about those stolen blueprints?"

"He has something on his mind; I've noticed it, too." Whit frowned. "I didn't want to say anything, but since you've brought it up, there is something else that bothers me. He's taken to walking in his sleep!"

Jackie almost dropped the plate. "Greg? Walking in his sleep?"

"Don't ask me to explain it." Whit shrugged. "I've been sleeping with one ear open ever since our burglary. I thought I heard noises several times before, but wrote it off when I couldn't find anyone prowling around. Then, last night I saw Greg."

"What was he doing?" Jackie asked eagerly.

"At first, he was monkeying around with the bulkheads — tapping them and pushing on them. After a while, he started pacing 'round and 'round the deck. Ten minutes later he came back to his bunk and stretched out, and he didn't budge for the rest of the night."

"Did he say anything?"

"Not a syllable. I trailed along behind him to make sure he didn't fall over the side, but I was too baffled to try to wake him. I don't think he believed me when I told him about it this morning. Said he'd never heard of such a crazy stunt."

"Something must be preying on his mind." Jackie frowned. "I've heard that people react strangely at times when they are troubled with a problem they can't solve."

Whit looked dubious. "Greg is the most normal guy I've ever known," he declared. "What possible problem could he have? He's healthy, he's going to marry the second prettiest girl in Santa Teresa, and he's about to join his dad in making a mint of money selling real estate."

"I didn't mean personal problems, exactly," Jackie murmured. "I meant — Whit, I can't get those blueprints out of my mind. I keep wondering who took them, and whether he has already succeeded in handing them over to the enemy. I'm sure Greg is worried about the same thing. More so, probably, because he was actually on the base when the plans were stolen."

"So was I — so were two thousand other sailors." Whit dragged a hand through his close-cropped red hair. "Holy smoke, Jackie!" he burst out. "Do you suppose Greg *knows* who took those blueprints?"

"Of course not," she said firmly. "If he did, he would have notified the FBI immediately. Remember, he said that as the Admiral's aide he stuck pretty close to that party of newsmen and photographers who were visiting the base? I think he has been going over and over their movements in his mind, trying to recall if one of them slipped away from the group for any length of time. He must feel partly responsible for the theft, even though no one could have foreseen that such a thing would happen. It's become sort of an obsession with him to expose the culprit."

"And that's what pressured him into climbing out of the sack in the middle of the night to go prowling around the boat?" Whit shook his head. "Sounds goofy to me."

"Listen!" Jackie cried. "Greg's theory hinged on the fact that he thought the blueprints were smuggled out of Port Dixon aboard the *Albatross*. Subconsciously, he might believe that they are still hidden somewhere on this boat!"

"He was poking at the bulkheads," Whit reflected. "Ah — they couldn't be, though.

This houseboat has been searched so many times it's practically threadbare!"

"I didn't say they were still here. I said Greg might *believe* they were," Jackie pointed out reasonably. "You'd better see if you can't get him interested in something else."

Whit promised to do what he could. "Want to go to a movie tomorrow night?" he asked, squeezing her hand as she started down the gangplank.

"I'd love to. Though by the time we're through chipping all that paint we may be too bleary-eyed to watch it." Jackie laughed. "See you at nine in the morning."

It was closer to ten o'clock, however, when Jackie arrived at the houseboat on Saturday morning. Immediately after breakfast, Fran Harris telephoned, and upon learning that Val was nowhere about, she proceeded to outline the plan she had in mind.

"I want to give Val a bridal shower," she confided. "Is next Saturday night all right with you?"

"Sure," Jackie answered. The same idea had occurred to her, but she lacked a place to hold the shower and still preserve the necessary secrecy. "What can I do to help?"

"Just make sure Val gets here without suspecting anything. I want it to be a real surprise. Tip off her fiancé so that he won't make any big plans for that evening."

They chatted a few minutes longer before hanging up. Then, after explaining to Mrs. Prescott that she would be away for the rest of the day, Jackie headed for the inlet. Whit greeted her enthusiastically and, when the paint chipping operation was completed in record time, complimented her on her workmanship.

"You're so good I think I'll let you paint, too," he told her.

"Thanks a million!" Jackie retorted, but she didn't really mind. Working side by side with Whit, chores she would ordinarily have classed as drudgery became almost pleasant.

They picnicked on chicken-filled pastries and frosty lemonade, and dabbled their toes in the cove's clear, shallow water before resuming work on the *Albatross*. During the afternoon, Whit finished sanding down the decks, while Jackie polished the portholes to a glistening sparkle.

"Wonder what happened here?" she murmured, catching her finger on a rough edge. The casement into which the porthole fitted was splintered. It looked as if it had been damaged at one time, and inexpertly repaired.

The grating hum of the sander drowned out her voice, however, and Whit failed to hear her comment. Shrugging, Jackie moved her cleaning equipment on to the next port-hole and promptly forgot about the splintery one adjoining it.

Contrary to her prediction, they both enjoyed the movie and the drive-in ham-burger which followed.

"My gosh, I almost forgot!" Whit exclaimed with a suddenness which almost caused Jackie to spill her malt. "I found a res-taurant that's going out of business. Heard about it from a fellow in the drugstore."

"Wonderful! Is it here in Santa Teresa?"

"No. It's down the coast about thirty miles. Little place called Amigos."

"Amigos — friends," Jackie translated. Many California towns bore the original names given them by the first Spanish set-tlers. "When do you plan on seeing the owner?"

"The sooner the better. We could drive down together, if you'd like to come." Whit had tapped his lean savings to purchase a small, secondhand car. "I'd take the *Albatross*, but I haven't a decent chart of these waters. Besides, the paper said there might be rain squalls."

Jackie agreed that the proposed excursion sounded like an ideal way to spend a Sunday. On the way home they speculated on what sort of place the Café El Gato might prove to be, and what sort of arrangement might be made with the owner for the sale of his equipment.

CHAPTER SEVEN

Shortly after noon the following day, Jackie and Whit set out along the barren coastal road. Although ominous-looking clouds glowered on the horizon, the predicted rain squalls did not materialize. Several times Jackie asked Whit to stop the car so that she might photograph some of the majestic rock formations which jutted up from the frothing surf.

"You shutterbugs!" Whit said indulgently as she clambered out on the ledge and teetered precariously while focusing on her target. "Anything for a good shot. You ought to get together with Rog Nelson, my partner. Now *there* is a camera addict. Never goes anywhere without a couple of bulging cases strapped over his shoulder. He looks like a tourist even in his own home town!"

Jackie stuck out her tongue at him and climbed back into the car. "He ought to have a grand collection by the time he returns from the Orient," she remarked, thinking vaguely of cherry trees and Balinese dancers.

"Right now, he's on destroyer duty, patrolling the passage between Formosa and Quemoy. Pretty much of a trouble spot over there. But last time he wrote they were about to start for home and he was hoping the ship would put in at Hong Kong and Tokyo long enough for him to shoot up a few yards of film."

Urged on by Jackie, Whit described some of the places he had visited during his hitch in the Navy. Almost before they knew it, the little car was toiling up the steep, winding road which led to Amigos.

The buildings which fronted the town's main street were ramshackle and unpainted. Few pedestrians were to be seen on the sidewalks. The gutters were clogged with debris, and the gloomy weather only intensified their impression that the place was really a ghost town and the sparse population figments of their imagination.

"Amigos looks a little short on friends at the moment," Jackie commented as Whit pulled up to the curb in front of the only whitewashed building they had seen so far.

A decal of a stalking black cat embellished the door of the café. When no one appeared to answer their tentative knock, Whit tried the latch. Finding it unlocked, they stepped

104

inside. Jackie was quick to notice the scrubbed appearance of the floors and counters, and that the furnishings were solid and unmarred.

A slender, black-haired boy of about sixteen emerged through the swinging door at that moment. Whit asked if he might speak with the proprietor, and the boy nodded shyly, answering that he would bring his uncle.

Manuel Rodriguez was a hospitable little man with a quick smile and a hearty handshake. "*Senor, senorita,* come in — my house is yours," he said, giving them the traditional Spanish greeting. "You will not mind coming into the kitchen? I am my own cook, and the food must be tended."

Seated in the homey room surrounded by penetrating odors of garlic, onion, and cheese, Whit stated his errand. *Senor* Rodriguez listened politely.

"I see. You weesh tables and chairs for this new business of yours." He smiled, white teeth flashing against his olive skin. "That is good. I must sell. The mill, you see, which gave work to most of the people in this town has gone — closed down. My customers went with it." He shrugged philosophically. "So my nephew, Felipe, and I go back to Guaymas."

While the two men discussed details of the sale, Jackie wandered over to the huge iron range and watched as Felipe stirred the contents of one bubbling pot, added a pinch of salt to another. With an amused grin, he reeled off the names of the dishes.

"Frijoles, tamales, enchiladas," he said. "You like them?"

"They smell wonderful," Jackie told him.

"You must dine with us, you and your friend."

Manuel Rodriguez promptly seconded the invitation. Jackie and Whit, their appetites whetted by the tantalizing aromas, readily accepted, and were doubly glad of the decision when at the close of the meal Felipe took up his guitar and began to strum the melodies of old Mexico.

"Why don't you hire Felipe to play on the *Albatross?*" Jackie asked dreamily. "Between his music and your cooking, you'd have to turn the cabins into extra dining rooms in no time."

"Good idea, but I'm afraid he is going back to Mexico with his uncle," Whit answered.

Felipe had been listening with interest. He would, he said, prefer to stay in California, at least for the rest of the summer. Had they a job for him?

"Not a very profitable one, I'm afraid,"

Whit said, explaining that his budget would make a shoestring look fat.

"But lots of tips, maybe?" Felipe grinned, his black eyes sparkling. "I sing and play the guitar. I clear the tables, I wash the dishes. You won't be sorry."

Whit promised to think it over and let the boy know in a week's time, when he would return with the *Albatross* to collect the furniture. He and Manuel Rodriguez had had no difficulty in coming to an agreement, and a receipted bill of sale was in his pocket when at last they left the Café El Gato.

Stepping out into the street was like wading into the soft center of a marshmallow. The gray-white fog obscured even the closest objects. Jackie clung tensely to the window handle while Whit cautiously maneuvered around the sharp curves and turns. Then, suddenly, they were able to see again. The fog was above them, hovering over the hill and the town of Amigos like a ceiling wispy with patches of flaking plaster.

"Scared?" Whit asked, removing his eyes from the road for the first time in fifteen minutes.

"Not now. I was, a little," Jackie admitted. Settling back, she closed her eyes. What a wonderful day it had been! Not even the fog could spoil it. With a warm feeling of happiness, she thought of the firelit kitchen, of Felipe's fingers whispering across the strings of his guitar to bring forth those poignant melodies.

"Oh Whit, thank you for bringing met" she cried. "I've never spent such a perfect day!"

The glow of the dashboard was their only illumination, but she could see his face light up with pleasure. "Neither have I," he agreed enthusiastically. "Your being along — well, it made all the difference." For a time, he drove in silence. Then he burst out, "It must be the very dickens being a Captain of Industry!"

Jackie stared at him. "What brought that on?"

"Even trying to get a small business like mine established takes nearly every minute I have."

"But think how nice it will be when the customers start flocking in."

"Guess you're right. Maybe then I'll be able to relax and concentrate on something really important." An alarming thought struck him. "You're not going to leave Santa Teresa once the wedding is over, are you?"

"It all depends. I — I hope not." More than ever Jackie dreaded the move back to the city. If only she could find an apartment!

The return journey consumed more than an hour. By the time they drove up to the

Prescott house, the sidewalks were deserted, and the only sign of life was the parade of yellow street lights glowing mistily through the darkness.

"Nobody home," Whit remarked, eyeing the darkened windows. "Gallivanters, these Prescotts. As bad as the Egans and Tor-rances."

"It's nearly ten." Jackie smiled as she looked at the dashboard clock. "They'll be home soon. Greg went with them to visit Val's grandparents."

Whit walked around to open the car door for her. "Just the same, I don't like —"

He stiffened, staring at the house.

Her fingers tightening over his, Jackie followed his gaze. A bulky shadow flickered away from the enclosure of the porch. An instant later, a form materialized, solidly, at the head of the driveway.

The man continued to move toward them, not pausing in his measured tread until he had reached the curb.

"You wouldn't," he said with more than a hint of truculence in his tone, "be Gregory Malden, would you?"

Jackie's heart resumed its normal beat. How silly, she thought shakily, to have been so afraid. As if, in Santa Teresa, there was anything to fear. As if, she added reluctantly, men like Alexei Litvinov still prowled the quiet streets.

"Nope," Whit said. "You wanted to see him?"

The stranger produced a wallet from his pocket and held it open in the flood of the street lamp. "He wanted to see me. Telephoned. Said it was urgent."

The man's picture and his name, Thomas J. Quinn, were stamped on his credentials. "Federal Bureau of Investigation," Jackie read. Wide-eyed, she met his unblinking gaze. "Oh, but there must be some mistake. Greg wouldn't —"

"Why don't we find out what this is all about?" Whit interjected quietly. "Let's go inside."

When they were seated in the living room, Whit introduced Jackie and himself, adding that they were close friends of Greg Malden. "You're with the FBI?" he asked.

"Special agent," said Thomas J. Quinn. "Can you tell me where to find Mr. Malden?"

Whit and Jackie exchanged glances. "As far as we know, he went visiting with his fiancée and her family," Jackie said. "I can telephone, if you like, and see if they are still there."

"Would you do that, please?" Although Mr. Quinn's words were pleasant, his voice had an authoritative ring.

She found the number in the desk directory, dialed, and exchanged a few sentences with someone at the other end of the wire.

"Mrs. Prescott said that Greg had been with them all day, but that he left rather suddenly around seven o'clock," Jackie relayed. "He insisted there was something important that he had to do. When Val's father offered to drive him home, Greg told him that he would take a taxi rather than spoil the evening for the rest of the family."

"Mr. Malden lives at this address?" Mr. Quinn asked.

Whit explained that Greg stayed with him aboard the *Albatross*. "We don't want to pry, sir, but you've got us sort of worried," he admitted. "You mentioned that Greg called you. Mind telling us why?"

"I'm not sure myself." Mr. Quinn looked thoughtfully from one to the other of them, until Jackie felt like squirming in discomfort.

Finally, seemingly satisfied with what he saw, he resumed: "At eight-five a call came in to our office from a person who said his name was Gregory Malden. He gave this address, and asked that an agent meet him as soon as possible at a houseboat which was anchored in a cove a few hundred yards down the hill behind the house. Mr. Malden said that he had discovered something of the greatest possible importance. However, he declined to reveal anything further over the telephone."

"And that's all?" Jackie cried.

"There *was* one other thing," the FBI man hesitantly admitted. "He chuckled, as though it were a joke of some kind, and said we needed a password so he would know who was approaching. When I got near the cove, he said, I should whistle 'Anchors Aweigh.'"

Mr. Quinn's grave expression was all that restrained Jackie from laughing aloud. The whole tale had sounded slightly ridiculous to begin with, but with this last statement, it took on a cloak-and-dagger aspect. Secret password! And a whistle at that!

Apparently, Whit shared her opinion. "I hate to say this, sir, but I've got a notion that someone was pulling your leg. Greg isn't a very imaginative guy — he couldn't dream up anything as mysterious as this in a hundred years!"

"Did you go down to the houseboat?" Jackie asked Mr. Quinn.

"Certainly," he affirmed. "We can't afford to pass up any leads. When Mr. Malden didn't meet me as promised, I took the liberty of looking through the cabins. Not a soul around anywhere. I waited for more than half an hour and then came back here to see if

112

someone else might know what this affair was all about."

"I'm awfully sorry," Whit mumbled. Abruptly, his expression changed from puzzlement to relief. A car had pulled into the driveway. "Perhaps the Prescotts can help you," he said hopefully as Val and her parents entered the house.

Listening to Mr. Quinn describe the enigmatic telephone call a second time, Jackie felt a gradual sense of unease steal over her. Supposing, she thought, the implausible story *were* true. Supposing it was Greg, and not some prankster, who had phoned the FBI? What possible reason could he have had for doing so — and why wasn't he here to explain?

". . . The Sunshine Cab Company," she emerged from her speculations to hear Mr. Prescott say.

While everyone sat frankly eavesdropping, Mr. Quinn placed a call to the taxi company and spoke briefly with the dispatcher.

"He came back here, all right," he reported, hanging up. "Each driver keeps a log of his fares. Mr. Malden paid off the cab at this address at 7:16 P.M. Roughly fifty minutes elapsed, therefore, between the time he arrived and the time he called me." The Federal agent looked quizzically at the Prescott

113

family. "Was there anything unusual about his behavior earlier in the day?"

Val, who had been sitting white-faced and tense throughout the recital, suddenly came to life.

"Yes," she said, straining to keep the tremor out of her voice. "He was — he was fine until we went out to mail some letters for Granddad shortly before dinner. Greg dropped the letters in the slot and then he stood there just staring at the mailbox, as if he'd never seen one before. I asked him what was the matter, and he said, 'Right under our noses the whole time and we never guessed!' He looked awfully excited, but he wouldn't explain what he meant. As soon as we had finished eating, he jumped up and said he had to go."

"I see." Mr. Quinn rose briskly and turned to Whit. "I want to have another look at that houseboat of yours. Could be I missed something."

Jackie had no intention of being excluded, although Mrs. Prescott insisted that she and Val would wait at the house for their return. Carrying powerful flashlights, Mr. Prescott and Whit strode down the overgrown trail to the inlet, while Jackie and Mr. Quinn followed closely behind.

The *Albatross* rocked serenely at anchor,

114

silent and deserted looking as any *Flying Dutchman*. Her phantom appearance soon changed, however, as lights flooded the creaky old boat and they began a thorough inspection of her decks and cabins.

It was Whit who discovered the damaged porthole. He had been raking his flashlight across the bulkheads and railings while the two older men concentrated on the boat's interior. With a muffled exclamation, he focused the beam on the chipped fragments of wood beneath the little round pane.

Mr. Quinn emerged hastily onto the deck in answer to Whit's shout. Jackie, watching him bend to inspect the damage, had a sudden, vivid recollection of a soapy sponge and herself industriously polishing portholes.

"That's the splintery one!" she cried. "I caught my finger on the rough edge and thought what a shoddy repair job someone had done."

Mr. Quinn demanded a full description of the porthole's former appearance, but Jackie could tell him nothing except that it had looked as if the wood below it was dented at one time and then haphazardly patched up. She was rather abashed at the furor her exclamation had caused.

"These marks are fresh," the Federal man commented thoughtfully. "I'd say that someone had been gouging here with a pen-knife. Notice the small crevice between the solid wooden frame and this plywood facing? A thin object could have been inserted here and the breach filled in with putty or some other substance."

"Oh!" Jackie gasped, and Whit, obviously struck with the same idea, echoed her startled cry.

"Oh, what?" Mr. Quinn snapped. "Come on — out with it!"

"This is all strictly guesswork, sir," Whit said hesitantly. "I'm sure your office must have been informed about the submarine blueprints which were stolen from the Port Dixon Naval Base?" He took a deep breath when the older man stiffened. "Well, Greg had a — a theory on how those blueprints could have been smuggled out . . ."

The night air seemed charged with tension as Whit recounted the details of Greg's idea. Mr. Quinn listened without interrupting, but his face was no longer impassive.

"Great Scott!" he ranted. "And you two characters just sat on this keg of dynamite without telling anyone?"

"We didn't really *know* anything," Whit protested. "It was just a notion that Greg had. If we had thought for one minute that the blueprints might still be aboard —"

116

"Okay, okay. You didn't want to stir up a hornet's nest of red tape without something more than a hunch to go on," Mr. Quinn said wearily. "Can't say I blame you, when you put it that way. It's too late now, of course."

"Mr. Quinn," Jackie choked, "what — what do you think happened to Greg?"

His refusal to meet her eyes was answer enough.

CHAPTER EIGHT

Jackie sat up instantly at the first raucous jangle of her alarm clock the next morning. For a few seconds she felt as if she were struggling out of the depths of a nightmare. All too soon, however, the events of the night before came flooding back. The nightmare, every horrible minute of it, had been real.

Mr. Quinn, catapulted into action by Whit's revelation, had called in a squad of city policemen to help search the underbrush and shoreline for some trace of the missing Greg. Throughout the long night, Jackie sat with Val at her bedroom window, watching flashlight beams methodically crisscross every foot of the thicket. But although she had remained at the window until the night's blackness was diluted by gray streaks of dawn, she had heard no cry of discovery, had seen no converging of lights and men at any point.

They hadn't found Greg.

"He'll show up," Jackie told herself fiercely.

118

"It's just morbid to believe that he was kidnapped."

But try as she might, she could think of no other explanation for Greg's mysterious disappearance. She realized now that his theory regarding the theft of the blueprints had been correct — in all but one vital detail. The blueprints *were* smuggled out of Port Dixon aboard the *Albatross*, but rather than reclaim them immediately, the spy, for some unknown reason, had left them in their original hiding place.

"Until last night," she murmured.

The fact that Greg had not discovered the documents until the very evening the spy had chosen to retrieve them seemed like a cruel twist of fate. Greg had searched the houseboat again and again, and undoubtedly had noticed the splintered frame beneath the porthole. But even his agile mind did not make the connection until he dropped a letter in a mailbox slot. Then he had put two and two together — and blundered into mortal danger.

Descending the stairs, Jackie found Whit and Mr. Prescott drooping over their coffee cups at the kitchen table. Lines of fatigue were etched across their faces and their tired eyes confirmed her guess that neither of them had slept.

"Any news?" she asked, forcing the words around the lump in her throat.

"Not a clue," Whit said disconsolately. "The police found some trampled footprints in the sand, but there's no way of telling who made them. Too blurred."

"Greg is a smart boy," Mr. Prescott said, trying to boost their morale. "He'll find a way to let us know where he is."

"Hope he lets me know personally. I'd like to get my hands on those thugs," Whit growled.

Jackie filled a coffee cup for herself and stirred it pensively. "What about enlisting the *Courier*'s aid?" she proposed. "They could run a photo of Greg and ask that anyone who knows of his whereabouts call Mr. Quinn or Chief Daley."

Whit's answer was an instantaneous "No!"

"That is one thing Mr. Quinn was most emphatic about," Mr. Prescott explained. "Any chance that Greg has of coming out of this predicament alive could be forfeited if there was the slightest whisper of publicity."

"The FBI is pretty sure that Greg wouldn't have admitted calling them," Whit added. "They're banking on the hope that the kidnappers will be lulled into a false sense of security when no further mention of the blueprints is made. If any sharp reporter were to connect Greg's disappearance with those sub plans, though —" He broke off and substituted a throat-cutting gesture for the rest of the sentence.

"Aren't they going to do *anything?*" Jackie asked angrily.

"They are already doing a great many things," Mr. Prescott assured her. "Every airport and seaport on the West Coast is under surveillance. Every out-of-the-way spot in this vicinity which might serve as a hide-out is being visited by Federal men in the guise of door-to-door salesmen. They're working day and night on this case, but under no circumstances must the country's security be jeopardized."

Jackie realized that there was much more at stake than the life of one man. Nevertheless, she feared that this policy of ultra discretion might cause a delay which could prove fatal to Greg.

"I guess Mr. Quinn knows best," she admitted with a sigh. "I won't breathe a word about it to anyone."

Whit walked with her to the bus stop. Worry showed in every plane of his face, but overshadowing the worry was a rugged look of determination. "Greg is my best friend," he said. "I'm not going to let anyone quit looking until they find him!"

Jackie had anticipated some trouble in keeping her promise to remain silent. The eagle-eyed reporters and cameramen with whom she worked had the ability to practically "smell" a scoop. As it turned out, though, the staff members were too much concerned with an internal crisis to pay any attention to her.

"Mr. MacFarland is on the warpath," Melinda confided in a whisper. "The *Herald* devoted almost half its front page to a statistical report on their circulation growth as opposed to our decline."

"How bad is it?" Jackie asked.

"It's not bad; it's second-degree murder! And to make things worse, we've lost one of our biggest advertisers to them. If this keeps up, the *Courier* will be the laughingstock of the newspaper industry!"

Almost afraid to look at it after this gloomy buildup, Jackie picked up a copy of the *Herald*. The disparity between the two newspapers' popularity was even wider than she had thought. Unless drastic and immediate steps were taken to halt the swing of *Courier* subscribers to the *Herald*, it appeared that the *Courier* would soon cease to be a competitor at all.

"I hope the boss has some bright ideas," she murmured apprehensively.

"He'd better, or he will be getting the axe along with the rest of us," Melinda predicted. "Did you see the notice? General meeting for all editorial staff members at eleven."

Bruce MacFarland had formulated several plans to revive reader interest, Jackie learned. Among these were wider sports coverage, three additions to the comic-strip page, the inauguration of an "inquiring reporter" column, and a variety of contests. Most of these moves were to be expected, but the summons which Jackie received ordering her to report to the Managing Editor's office following the meeting came as a total surprise.

"I'm taking you off 'Society,'" Mr. MacFarland announced. "For part of the day, at least. You're going to do the 'inquiring reporter' column."

Jackie could not have more astonished if he had proclaimed that she was slated to be the first girl into space.

"Th-that's grand! Thank you," she stammered, realizing that the words were inadequate, but too stunned to think of a more suitable reply.

"Surprised?" he asked with the grimace he used for a smile. "I'm giving you a crack at the job for two reasons. Miss Foster won't be needing a full-time assistant during the slack vacation season — and there's nobody else I can spare to take it on."

In a more businesslike tone, Jackie asked, "What does an 'inquiring reporter' inquire about?"

He shoved a sheet of paper headed "Question of the Day" across the desk. "These. One a day. You pick out a street corner and ask a dozen people the same question. If their answers don't have enough variety, you ask a dozen more. I'll assign a photographer to go along with you."

Still unable to believe her good fortune, Jackie took the list of questions and ran to tell Melinda of her part-time promotion. Later that afternoon, her telephone jingled and Don George said, "Inquiring reporter? This is the inquiring cameraman. Are you ready to inquire?"

Jackie laughed. "Ready and willing. Meet you downstairs."

The first question of the day was a controversial one, regarding a proposed bond issue in the coming city elections. Jackie, scribbling frantically while Don snapped his pictures, recorded twelve different replies from the first dozen people she queried. There was no need to go on to a second dozen.

"Do you know what one of the contests is going to be?" Don asked as they trudged back to the *Courier* building. "The 'mystery pedestrian.' I'm supposed to make myself practically invisible and aim the camera at a mob of people in the street. Next day when the paper comes out one of the heads in the photo is circled. Cries the *Courier*, 'Who is the mystery pedestrian?' If he shows up at the advertising booth by two o'clock, he's given five dollars."

"What if he doesn't?"

"Then we've found another poor, misguided soul who doesn't read the *Courier*. His five bucks is added to the next day's winnings."

"I should think the chance of winning a prize would stimulate circulation," Jackie said hopefully. She transcribed her notes in record time and managed to have the copy in final form by five o'clock. Taking her seat on the bus, she remembered guiltily that she had not thought of Greg Malden for almost three hours.

Would they — could they have found him?

Jackie crossed her fingers. "Maybe he'll be there when I get home," she told herself.

But when Jackie walked in the door one look at Val's face told her that no such miracle had occurred. One of Mr. Quinn's assistants reported with almost monotonous regularity; however, the FBI had so far failed to come up with a single lead.

"Nobody can simply vanish into thin air," Whit exclaimed that evening. "With all their technical know-how and trained agents, they've got to turn up a trace of Greg sooner or later."

How much "later" would be too late? Jackie wondered, and then could have kicked herself for letting such pessimistic notions wander into her head. Of course the FBI would find Greg — and soon!

"Val is being awfully brave about everything," she said admiringly. "If Greg were my fiancé, I'd probably be paddling around in my own tears, but she keeps insisting that he will show up before the seventeenth."

"She isn't postponing the wedding plans?" Whit asked, surprised.

"Oh, no. She — she has so much faith in him, it's positively heartbreaking. I've never known anyone with such courage." Jackie was close to tears. "Oh, Whit, I'm so afraid! For Greg, and for Val, too. If something dreadful has happened to him —"

"Stop it!" he said sharply. "Haven't you ever heard of positive thinking?"

Ashamed of her outburst, Jackie nevertheless guessed that Whit was also finding it hard to keep from dwelling on the bleakness of the situation.

"You're right," she declared. "Anything

Val can do, we should at least be able to imitate. She has her faith in Greg — I'm placing my trust in Thomas J. Quinn!"

But however capable, the Federal agent was no magician. Day by day, hopes for Greg's rescue and the recovery of the blueprints waned still further. Although the others struggled with grim determination to remain optimistic, by Thursday Val was the only one whose faith remained unshaken.

"I just *know* everything is going to be all right, Mother," she said quietly, when urged to announce a postponement of the wedding.

Val could not keep the worry from showing in her eyes, though, and for the first time Jackie understood her friend's refusal to alter a single plan. To do so would be to admit that their worst fears might be true.

More than ever Jackie was grateful to Mr. MacFarland for assigning her to the inquiring reporter "beat." The heavy work load he had placed on her was exhausting but never dull, and by far the greatest blessing of her involved and varied duties was that she had very little time to brood over the fate of Greg Malden.

Much to his chagrin, Whit had been forbidden by Mr. Quinn to take any active part in the search for Greg. The Federal man had pointed out that the kidnappers would surely recognize him at once, while his own men worked under the cloak of anonymity.

"He said the spy had probably been watching the boat for days," Whit grumbled to Jackie on Thursday evening. Mr. and Mrs. Prescott had taken Val out for a drive, and the two had the living room to themselves.

Jackie was sympathetic, but practical. "I'm sure Mr. Quinn is right, Whit. If you were to start pounding on doors, the spy might be stampeded into taking some drastic action."

Whit continued to pace up and down. "There must be something we can do!" he burst out explosively.

In an effort to coax him into sitting down, Jackie reached for a copy of the *Courier*, which lay on an end table.

"All the new features have brought in sixty new subscribers already this week," she said with a touch of pride. "That doesn't sound like many, but it's a start. How do you like our 'Question of the Day' column?"

"Haven't seen it," Whit confessed sheepishly. "I've even been neglecting the *Albatross*. Can't seem to concentrate on anything lately."

He skimmed through the column. To Jackie's relief, the hint of a smile touched his lips as he read the dozen responses evoked by the Wednesday question of the day: "How

Henpecked Are Husbands?"

"Pretty good," he acknowledged. "A few more items in this vein might make the *Herald* start gnashing its teeth. Photographing the people who answer the questions is a swell idea. Who wouldn't buy a newspaper that had his picture in it?"

"The contests are our biggest subscription drawing card," she told him. "The Sports Editor received hundreds of replies to the first week's baseball quiz."

She flipped through the pages. "Here is Don's 'mystery pedestrian' photo. It's a beautiful shot — not at all blurred. He must have disguised himself as a tree or something."

Whit peered over her shoulder. "Uh-huh," he murmured appreciatively. "Good man with a lens."

"I'll show you what they've done to the sports page," Jackie began, but before she could turn the page, Whit had snatched the paper from her and was holding it under the light for a closer inspection.

"I *thought* there was something familiar looking about that guy!" he exclaimed.

It was Jackie's turn to crane her neck. "Who? The 'mystery pedestrian'?"

"No, this fellow standing on the fringes of the crowd." Whit pointed out the man. "He's turned at an angle, but you can see most of his face."

"One of your friends?" Jackie asked, wondering at his excitement.

"Not on your life!" Whit seemed unable to wrench his eyes from the half-shaded face in the photograph. "That's *Buck Younger!*"

There was no mistaking that pugnacious expression, he insisted, or the square, stony jaw thrust belligerently out toward the person to whom Buck was speaking.

"Oh, Whit, do you realize what this could mean?" Jackie gasped. "Greg was positive that Buck Younger collaborated with the spy in stealing the blueprints. He might have been in on the kidnapping, too!"

"And if Buck was in Santa Teresa yesterday, his hide-out can't be far away!" Whit groaned. "If only the photo were a half-inch wider, we could get a look at the man Buck was talking to. You can just see his shoulder and part of his arm."

Jackie admitted that for identification purposes this was very little to go on. "Oh!" she cried suddenly. "The negative! Don might have masked off the edges of it and printed only the main portion showing the 'mystery pedestrian'!"

Whit nearly knocked over a lamp in his dive for the telephone book. "Call him, quick!

This could break the whole case. Buck wouldn't have risked coming in to town just to see the sights. The other man in the picture *has* to be the spy!"

With trembling fingers, Jackie paged through to the "G's," and hunted until she found a listing for George, Donald. Whit held the phone while she dialed. Gradually the anticipation on their faces dissolved into disappointment as the steady ringing went unanswered.

"I'll try the *Courier*," Jackie said, determined to call every place in town, if necessary, to track down the cameraman. "I remember Don mentioning that he occasionally uses the darkroom in the evenings."

Unaware that she was holding her breath, she waited while the switchboard operator relayed the call to Don's extension. Once again, the intermittent buzzes aroused no answering voice.

"What rotten luck!" Whit growled as she held the receiver away from her ear so that he, too, could listen.

Jackie started to hang up. The phone was inches away from its cradle when a break in the monotonous buzzing made her tighten her grasp on the receiver. Swiftly, she raised the instrument to her ear.

" 'Lo," said a muffled, faraway voice.

"Don! Is that you?" Jackie cried.

"Yeah. Yeah, I think so," said the voice after a painful pause. "Be a good kid and — and call a doctor, will you? Somebody darn near caved my skull in!"

CHAPTER NINE

Jackie and Whit arrived at the *Courier* building minutes ahead of the ambulance, having delayed only long enough to summon a doctor and place a hasty call to Mr. Quinn. Clattering up the stairs, they wrenched open the door to the photographic department and halted just inside.

Stethoscope dangling from his ears, a sober-faced man swung around to face them. He motioned curtly for silence.

"Don!" Jackie stifled the exclamation as her eyes fell on the figure sprawled across the floor. "He isn't —"

"Concussion." The doctor's voice was a whisper. "Not too serious, probably, but I won't be able to tell with any degree of certainty until we get him to a hospital. Are you the person who called me?"

Jackie nodded, a tide of relief flooding over her.

In a moment, her weak-kneed sensation ebbed. Glancing around the room, she caught sight of the telephone receiver hanging limply from its cord. It must have taken every ounce of Don's strength to utter those few words. Once he had gasped out his plea for help, he had collapsed, too weak even to replace the phone.

She did so now, moving carefully around Don's motionless form. Whit came up beside her, pointing, and Jackie's startled gaze fastened on the open door of the darkroom.

It was a darkroom that was no longer dark. Light spilled from a harsh overhead globe, glinting on the shiny surfaces of a thousand negatives strewn about the room.

"Looks as if someone wanted his arm and shoulder to remain anonymous," Whit said tightly.

"I'm afraid so." As usual, they were one step behind their diabolically clever adversary. She gestured helplessly at the litter which swamped the darkroom. "How desperate he must have been, to attack Don and —"

"Didn't see him." Thick and halting, the cameraman's words were barely audible. "Bending over. Hit me . . ."

"You mustn't talk," the doctor interrupted. He motioned for the two white-clad men who had appeared in the doorway to hurry with the stretcher. Within seconds they had whisked their inert patient from the room. Below in the street the wail of a siren receded screamingly into the night.

A pair of city policemen wedged into the room, their eyes busily taking in details. Whit, recognizing them as two of the men who had helped search the thicket for Greg the previous Sunday, confided that Mr. Quinn was on his way and asked them to prevent anyone from tampering with the darkroom until the Federal agent had had an opportunity to dust it for fingerprints.

At the entrance of the building a throng of curious onlookers stirred expectantly as the police cordon opened to allow Whit and Jackie to pass through. Ignoring the inquisitive stares, they hurried to the car.

They had driven only a few blocks when a speeding sedan crowned by a flashing red beacon whipped past them. Jackie sighed thankfully, glimpsing a familiar gray slouch hat in the back seat. Somewhere in the disordered darkroom there might lie a clue. If so, Mr. Quinn would find it.

"Did you tell him about the photograph?" she asked. She had gone for her coat while Whit telephoned the Federal officer.

With a pained expression, Whit massaged his ear. "Yes, and you should have heard him. A Geiger counter being introduced to an atom bomb couldn't have made such a racket. He's positive that Buck Younger is in this up to his neck."

"I suppose that negative is burnt to a cinder by this time," Jackie said gloomily. "The spy couldn't risk being seen consorting with a known fugitive. He must have nearly died of apoplexy when that picture appeared in the paper."

"He's a daring bird," Whit muttered. "He must have found out earlier in the day where the darkroom was situated. As soon as the staff left for the night, he barged right in."

"And struck so fast and ruthlessly that poor Don didn't even have a chance to turn around." Thoughtfully, Jackie considered the assailant's audacity. Like an old nemesis, the point which had troubled her from the beginning of this strange affair returned to plague her anew. They were driving down a quiet side street; on an impulse, she asked Whit to pull in to the curb.

"Val and her folks will be home by now. I'd just as soon not discuss this in front of them," she explained.

"Okay by me. Got any new ideas?" Whit asked hopefully. "All of mine have ruts worn in them."

"Not new, exactly," she answered with a frown. "But for the first time, I've started

136

thinking of the spy as a real person, not just a — a sort of mechanical bogeyman. You said he was daring, and I certainly agree. Almost everything he's done has a distinct flavor of derring-do about it, a rashness that defies common sense. He's bold and fearless, and a genius at carrying out his decisions on a split-second timetable. Look at how he stole the blueprints! And tonight, the way he went after that negative."

"So he's a decisive fellow." Whit shrugged. "What's so perplexing about that?"

"Nothing, except that I can't understand why he stepped out of character at one crucial point. Why did he dillydally around for weeks while the blueprints mildewed on the *Albatross*?"

"I thought you must be leading up to something." Whit eyed her with dawning admiration. "You *do* put those little gray cells to work, don't you? Hummm. My guess would be that he needed time to set up a deal with a prospective buyer."

"Ye-es," Jackie said dubiously. "I suppose it wasn't really such a great risk, leaving the blueprints where they were. After all, Lance Shelby didn't use the houseboat very often. Most of the time the *Albatross* stayed in port where the spy could keep a sharp eye on her. And it was less hazardous than if he'd hidden them in his own house — if he were suspected, there would be no evidence to convict him. But I keep picturing him as a man who enjoys flirting with danger. This one act is completely inconsistent."

"Maybe he planned to go back for that new radar device," Whit blurted, and then looked as if he could have bitten his tongue out.

Jackie spun around, her eyes wide and incredulous. "What!"

"I ought to be muzzled," Whit said weakly.

"Not so fast, Mr. Whitney Egan. What was that about a new radar device?"

"Shhh! Jackie, it's just scuttlebutt — gossip. I don't even know for sure that there is such a thing."

These protestations did not deceive her for a minute. It would have been almost impossible to keep some hint of a tremendous new defensive weapon from leaking out on a base as large as Port Dixon. While the "scuttlebutt" might not be wholly accurate, it was undoubtedly rooted in fact. And if the spy had been alert enough to ferret out the location of the submarine blueprints, a few adroitly placed questions could have revealed to him the existence of this even more valuable invention.

"Oh, Whit," she breathed. "Think of what a foreign power would pay if he got that, as well as the blueprints. The spy could retire for life!"

"Come off it, Jackie! He wouldn't be fool-hardy enough to go back a second time. That wouldn't be boldness — it would be hara-kiri!"

"Not necessarily. In the first place, nobody knows who the spy is. He could be anyone! And how many people are supposed to know about the — the new thing? I'll bet you're not. The authorities would never suspect that he had found out about it, let alone dream that he'd be audacious enough to try to steal it. The odds against such a maneuver could work in his favor."

Whit wavered, his thoughts trapped on a pendulum which swung between his own conviction that the feat would be impossible and Jackie's convincing arguments to the contrary.

"Boy, am I confused!" he muttered. "Here I thought civilian life would be nice and uncomplicated. I couldn't go back to a quiet little ranch in Montana, oh, no. I had to buy a houseboat and settle in a hotbed of interna-tional intrigue like Santa Teresa!"

Jackie changed her tactics. "I'm sorry," she said contritely. "You're probably right. I don't imagine the spy ever wants to go within a hundred miles of Port Dixon again."

Unexpectedly, Whit grinned. "You're going to back down and let me take the initiative, now that you have me nicely riled up about this notion, is that it? Women!"

A look of mischief danced across Jackie's face. "You'll call Mr. Quinn?"

"Of course I'll call Mr. Quinn." Still shaking his head, Whit reached for the ignition key. "There's about one chance in a million that your idea is on the nose, but it's a chance I don't want to be responsible for. The FBI might want to have the — the thing shipped back to Washington until our shifty adversary is behind bars.

"And if you're wrong," he concluded, "I think I'll throttle you!"

The temporary loss of Don George from the *Courier*'s staff threw an extra work load onto his fellow cameramen. Don was so well liked, though, that the additional assignments were willingly accepted, and most of the newspaper's personnel even juggled their busy schedules in order to visit him in the hospital.

Shortly before noon on the Friday following Don's attack, Lance Shelby appeared at the door of the City Room. He announced his intention of stopping by the hospital during the noon hour.

"Would you girls care to go along on an errand of mercy?" he asked them.

Jackie glanced hopefully at Melinda, who nodded.

"Of course! Why don't you ask Ted Rigney to come along, too?" the Society Editor suggested. "He and I have a meeting to cover at that end of town this afternoon. You can drop us off at the auditorium on the way back."

Jackie found the hushed atmosphere of the hospital depressing, especially after a stern-faced nurse cautioned them to confine their visit to fifteen minutes and to avoid exciting the patient.

Don lay flat, his face almost as white as the bandage which swathed his head. Nevertheless, he insisted that he would be back on the job within a few days. His main reaction to the attack was one of anger.

"If I ever find the guy who hit me, I'll pulverize him with his own blackjack," he threatened darkly.

"You haven't *any* idea of what he looked like?" Lance probed.

"No, he must move like a cat. I didn't even hear him." Don glared belligerently at the circle of faces surrounding his bed. "Well, how was I supposed to know somebody was going to sneak in and conk me over the head? Why pick on me?"

141

"Easy!" Ted warned. "They'll throw us out of here if you start hollering. Lance was just offering to head a vigilante committee in case you could point out the varmint. None of us likes this any better than you do."

"I'll bet it was one of those clowns from the *Herald*, jealous because we're finally getting back some of our own business," Melinda declared. "Do the police have a lead yet?"

"Not that they confided to me," Don grumbled. "I doubt it, though. Every cop in town must have been in here last night, spouting questions. Some who weren't exactly cops, too."

"What do you mean?" Lance asked quickly.

Don started to shake his head, then thought better of it. "They were asking the questions, not answering them. Maybe the district attorney's office got in on the act. I never saw them before, and they didn't bother to introduce themselves."

Jackie, who had been listening apprehensively, exhaled in relief. How wise of Mr. Quinn to keep his identity unknown. A hint to any of these inquisitive newshounds that the Federal authorities were involved could have landed the case on the front page. And that, she thought with a gasp, would have been the end of Greg Malden!

Ted carefully refrained from mentioning the damage to the irreplaceable negatives, fearing that the knowledge of their destruction would only excite Don further. Instead, he urged the young cameraman to relax and enjoy all the service and attention while he had the chance.

"It won't be long before you're back in the clutches of slave-driving MacFarland," he added.

A short time later, the four left the hospital, and after depositing Melinda and Ted at the door of the auditorium, Lance invited Jackie to lunch with him.

"I'll have time for a quick sandwich," she told him.

This was the first overture of friendliness the star reporter had made since their abbreviated dinner date at Pietro's. Jackie wondered whether an ulterior motive lay behind the invitation. Lance seldom did anything without a reason.

Almost as soon as they had seated themselves in the drugstore booth, she found that her hunch was correct.

"How did you and that redheaded swabbie happen to be on the scene last night?" he asked. "Don't tell me you have an inside track with the Demon of the Darkroom?"

Jackie realized that his highly trained senses

143

of observation were operating at full speed. She couldn't afford a single careless word!

"Looking for another scoop, Mr. Shelby?"

"A reporter's life isn't all fabulous trips to the Orient," he admitted. "Have to fit in a few slices of bread and butter once in a while, to go along with the cake."

Jackie pulled a napkin from the dispenser. "Blind luck, that's all," she said finally, deciding that to tell the truth with certain vital omissions would be her wisest course. "I telephoned Don, meaning to ask him about the pictures he had taken for one of our features. I guess the constant ringing of the phone must have restored him to consciousness. He answered just as I was about to hang up, and managed to gasp out a few words about needing a doctor."

Lance seemed unconvinced. "You were home and yet you came all the way back into town?" he said skeptically. "Why?"

Irritation at the cross-examination showed in her voice. "Because Don is my friend. I didn't know what had happened to him, but I wanted to be there in case I could help. He might have been dying!"

"Everyone sure is touchy today," Lance complained. "First Don explodes in my face, and now you!"

Jackie felt like telling him to stick to cake if

144

he didn't care for the commonplace bread and butter his attempts to pump her had evoked. Instead, she thanked him politely for the grilled cheese, reminding herself that he was only doing his job. Given his driving ambition to gain a story whatever the cost, it was only natural that Lance would try to ferret out all the details behind the assault on Don.

I suppose all's fair in love and newspaper reporting, she thought grudgingly. But I don't have to like it!

The bridal shower that Fran Harris had planned presented another problem. Like everyone outside of the immediate family and a few close friends, like Jackie and Whit, Fran knew nothing of Greg's disappearance. Jackie, balancing conscience against intuition, could not decide whether to spoil Fran's surprise by telling Val in advance, or whether to risk the possibility that her friend might find the party one shock too many. After an almost sleepless night, she came to the conclusion that Val should be forewarned of the surprise which lay in store for her.

"It doesn't seem quite fair to Fran," she concluded guiltily on Saturday morning. "But I was afraid —"

"That I might go into hysterics?" Val's

145

ghost of a smile was rueful; the tiny blonde girl appeared to have lost ten pounds in the past week. "I'm glad you understand. I'm not sure that even Mother realizes how I feel. If I let myself think for one minute that Greg mightn't be coming back, I'd probably just stand around screaming. But he *will* come back, Jackie; he *is* alive and well. I must keep on believing that!"

"Of course you believe it — and so do I!" Jackie asserted in nervous desperation. "Then it's all right — about tonight?"

"I'll go set my hair," Val answered.

"And Val sat there like a regular trooper for three full hours," Jackie told Whit the next morning. "I don't know where she found the courage. The presents were things for their new home, and she opened them and thanked people — and all the time she doesn't even know if Greg is alive or dead. I could have bawled."

"Val is a brave girl," Whit agreed soberly. "But don't forget there is a full week left before the wedding. Remember our resolution to trust Thomas J. Quinn."

She hadn't forgotten. "This business about the negative proves the spy hasn't left town yet, anyway," she said, plucking a sunbeam from the storm clouds which had burgeoned so menacingly seven days before. A thought suddenly struck her. "There's that inconsistency again. He's waiting, just as he waited before retrieving the blueprints. If we only knew why!"

"Maybe the dragnet is spread too wide," Whit guessed. "He's standing pat until the FBI relaxes its guard over the airports so he can board his flight to Moscow."

The ceaseless worry and speculation over Greg and the blueprints had dropped their morale to an all-time low. Jackie was thankful when Whit changed the subject.

"Any answers to your want ad for an apartment yet?"

"Two. Both far too expensive for a humble working girl. I'm still hoping that someone who knows the meaning of the word 'reasonable' will call."

He grinned. "Say, I've thought of just the place for you. Of course the commuting would be a little rough."

"Where?" Jackie asked eagerly.

"Amigos! I'll bet you wouldn't have any trouble finding a vacant apartment there, but as I said —" He ducked, narrowly avoiding the scrub brush which came hurtling across the deck. "Okay, okay! I was only trying to be helpful."

"Whimsical Whit! By the way, have you decided to hire Felipe?"

From his quick response, Jackie knew that he had given the matter a great deal of thought. "He'd be a tremendous asset, no doubt about that. I'm going to make him the best offer I can afford."

She smiled, happy to hear that the pleasant, nimble-fingered lad was to be one of the *Albatross'* unofficial "crew." She would be very much surprised if the customers didn't flock to hear the young guitarist.

Whit brought out a tides table and a navigational chart of the coastal waters which he had obtained from the Coast Guard.

"I told *Senor* Rodriguez I'd be down to pick up the furniture today. We'd better plan to leave at noon on the flood tide. Figure two hours each way and another couple hours to load the furniture — we can easily make it back before dark."

Jackie glanced at her wristwatch. Forty-five minutes remained before departure time.

"I'll run up to the house and pack a lunch," she proposed. "Is it all right if I invite Val to come along? A change of scenery might do her good."

"Sure, but hurry up," Whit cautioned. "We have to make that tide."

She scrambled up the path and through the back door. Her efforts to persuade her friend to accompany them on the outing proved futile, however. Val doggedly insisted on remaining near the phone in case some word about Greg should come.

Juggling a picnic kit crammed with sandwiches and a six-pack of Coca-Cola, Jackie hastened back to the inlet. "Made it with five minutes to spare," she panted. "Hope you like salami and pickles."

Whit nodded his approval and prepared to cast off. Jackie helped free the lines binding the *Albatross* to shore, then stood back while he turned the winch which would haul up the anchor. "Anchors aweigh, my boys . . ." A few bars of the Navy hymn flitted through her mind.

Greg's password, she thought as Mr. Quinn's account of Greg Malden's last telephone call recurred to her.

"He chuckled as if it were a joke of some kind. When I got near the cove, he said, I should whistle 'Anchors Aweigh.' "

Why should Greg have chuckled? Finding the blueprints was no joking matter. And why had he chosen that particular "password"? Association, she supposed; Greg as a former Naval officer had probably loved the song.

Or had they, she wondered suddenly, in all the excitement surrounding Greg's disappearance, overlooked something?

"None of us gave that remark another

thought," she told herself. "And yet it might —"

Jerking herself back to reality, Jackie turned to stare at the massive chain. It rose slowly, clankingly, reluctantly.

Link by link by link the chain dripped clear of the water until, af ter what seemed to Jackie an eternity spent with the winch's whine in her ears, the dark bow of the anchor itself emerged.

The anchor and, tightly wired to the leaden weight, a waterproof pouch.

CHAPTER TEN

"It's not possible," Jackie breathed incredulously. "It is simply not possible!"

A look of utter stupefaction had spread over Whit's face. Motionless as a pair of statues, neither he nor Jackie seemed able to move toward the object which held their rapt attention.

A long sixty seconds crawled by, the silence broken only by the steady drip, drip, drip of water, which snaked along the brine-encrusted chain and anchor and thick, oily surface of the pouch to dimple the cove in a widening series of circles.

It was the *Albatross* that prodded them into action. With nothing to link her to shore, she slid out on the rushing current of the tide. The sudden lurch dispelled their inertia. Whit jumped to throw the engine into reverse, while Jackie, her fingers tingling with excitement, bent and twisted at the strong wire which bound the pouch to the anchor.

"Hurry!" Whit called as her hand skidded

on the slimy, seaweed-coated oilskin.

Jackie cast a look of terror at the reef which loomed between them and the open sea, and plucked frantically at the wire. The engine hadn't caught. Without the dragging anchor to hold them back, the tide would propel them directly onto the boulders!

Miraculously, the final twist had freed it. The pouch spurted to the deck at the same instant that Whit dived toward the winch. The anchor and its clanking chain plunged viciously downward, barbing into the ocean floor and halting their forward progress with a snap which set Jackie reeling to the rail. Floundering after the pouch, Whit captured it in a flying tackle, scraping elbows and knees as the *Albatross* shuddered to a standstill.

"Close," he puffed. "Awfully close. This thing is as slippery as a slab of raw liver!"

Jackie peered down at the frothing surf and then hastily looked away. Mere yards separated them from the first gigantic rock!

They regained their balance and hobbled together into the cabin where they would be safe from prying eyes.

"If this is what I think it is," Whit said, "we could be in trouble."

Jackie laughed shakily. "What's trouble? I'm slated to die of old age pretty soon, anyway. Another day like today might just do it."

Eyeing the faded yellow oilskin, patched with brownish flakes of seaweed, Whit gingerly undid the flap. He drew out a long, cylindrical roll of papers. Jackie caught a glimpse of blue background, of sleek lines and precise figures before his brown fists snapped tight on the roll and secured it with a rubber band.

"Yup, we're in trouble," he confirmed. "Now what?"

There must, Jackie knew, be no postponement of the decision. Not so much as a minute could be wasted. The *Albatross* was not equipped with ship-to-shore telephone. One of them would have to chance swimming to shore.

Whit had come to the same conclusion. He bent to untie his shoes. "I'm going to leave you here for a few minutes," he began, but Jackie interrupted.

"No, I'll go. Be practical, Whit," she insisted. "I could never pilot the *Albatross* around those boulders, and that's exactly what you'll have to do unless I make it back here within half an hour. Take her out into deep water and head for the nearest Coast Guard station."

The stubborn line of his jaw relaxed slowly as he realized that her plan was their best means of safeguarding the precious blueprints. Thrusting the paper roll back into its pouch, he left the cabin and stood for a long moment reconnoitering the coastline. Ashore there was no sign of life except a faint stirring of leaves and shrubbery as the breeze rustled through the thicket.

Even then, he might not have agreed to her going had Jackie not taken the initiative. She removed her shoes before tiptoeing across the deck. While Whit's eyes still probed for menacing shapes beyond, she clambered onto the rail.

"Back soon!" she called.

Jackie cut the water in a clean, smooth dive. Bobbing to the surface, she struck out for shore a hundred yards away. Her sleeveless blouse and cotton slacks clung to her skin and she was grateful now that she had not succumbed to the temptation of wearing her new sundress. Its flaring skirt and binding straps would have been dangerous impediments for a swimmer.

The shallows were soon reached, and with water gushing from her hair and clothing, Jackie waded onto the sand. As she turned to wave, she saw that the *Albatross* lay almost directly in the center of the channel. If an attack should come, Whit would have ample warning.

From her own standpoint, though, the

thought was hardly comforting. Jackie wished that she could retreat into the water and dash back to the comparative safety of the houseboat, but stubbornly, she forced this cowardly notion from her mind.

"Well, go on. There's no reason to be afraid," she chided herself.

Would they — the spy and his accomplice — have continued to watch the houseboat even after their capture of Greg? Try as she would, Jackie could not repress the feeling that hostile eyes followed her every move. Resisting the impulse to peer back over her shoulder, she concentrated on Greg.

He, too, must have sensed that he was being watched. Otherwise, he would not have switched the blueprints to a safer hiding place. He had chosen it well, knowing that Whit would eventually hoist the anchor and find the pouch. Undoubtedly he had made the transfer while the spy's lookout had run to summon assistance.

Shivering, she wondered what story he had concocted to hide the truth. He must have offered some fairly plausible explanation for the blueprints' disappearance from the porthole. Of course, Greg might not have had time to say anything. He could have been — permanently silenced. But somehow, Jackie doubted this. She felt certain that behind

Greg's kidnapping lay a hard, practical purpose.

With a sob of thanksgiving, she burst through the garden gate. Stopping only long enough to slam and bolt the kitchen door, she snatched up the phone and dialed the now-familiar number.

Mr. Quinn would not ordinarily have been in his office on a Sunday. This afternoon, to Jackie's heartfelt relief, he was. The dispatch with which he responded to her appeal was gratifying. He would arrive within the hour, he assured her; in the meantime, no one was to take any action which might again place the blueprints in jeopardy.

Remembering her promise to return to the inlet, Jackie nevertheless had no desire to walk through the secluded grove alone a second time. Fortunately, Mr. Prescott was at home, and after hearing a brief summary of events, he agreed to escort her back to the water's edge.

"You are absolutely certain this is what you found?" His normally ruddy face had grown pale with concern.

"Yes. Whit knew at once," she replied. "It's baffling, I know, but for some reason Greg must have felt that danger was near and he did his best to safeguard the plans. I think he tried to give Mr. Quinn a clue when he mentioned 'Anchors Aweigh,' but of course he couldn't risk saying anything more over the telephone."

From the *Albatross* came a faint "halloo" as Whit spotted them. They called in return and sat down to wait.

"I must have your solemn pledge that none of you will reveal the whereabouts of these documents," Mr. Quinn said.

"Not even to my daughter?" Mr. Prescott asked. "This — this uncertainty has been a tremendous strain on Val."

The Federal agent nodded understandingly. "You may use your own discretion about telling your wife and daughter," he decided. "However, it is imperative that the news go no further. Actually, I imagine that Miss Prescott's primary concern is for her fiancé. The recovery of these papers tends to make his disappearance seem all the more mystifying."

"Do you think they intend using Greg to get back the blueprints?" Jackie couldn't help asking.

Mr. Quinn sighed wearily. "I would very much like to know the answer to that question myself," he said, adding that the unexpected discovery of the blueprints would by no means lessen the intensity of the search for

Greg. The FBI would continue its manhunt until every hope had been exhausted.

By the time Mr. Quinn and his men had departed, the flood tide on which Whit had intended to sail had ebbed. He was forced to postpone the trip to Amigos until the next day. Disappointed that she would be unable to accompany him in the excursion, Jackie promised to stop by the houseboat after work on Monday. She was nearly as eager as Whit to have another look at the furnishings which would serve the future customers of the *Albatross*.

Soft, vibrant chords struck from a guitar lilted across the water as she approached the inlet the following afternoon. So Felipe had agreed to come! That *was* good news, Jackie thought, quickening her steps. To her mind, the presence of the talented young musician all but assured the success of the new business venture.

"Had a postcard from Rog Nelson today," Whit said, after Jackie had greeted Felipe warmly and accepted a glass of iced tea. "He and another buddy of ours will be rolling into Santa Teresa in a few days. Their ship, the *Hudson*, berthed at Port Dixon over the weekend, and they'll pick up their discharges on Thursday."

"Super! Now that you have a few assistants,

I can stop scrubbing," Jackie smiled. She caught sight of the great pile of furniture stacked at one end of the deck. "How does our junior *Queen Mary* look in her new accessories?"

"Just exactly enough tables and chairs," Whit declared, proud of his accurate calculations. "Felipe's uncle threw in a stack of tablecloths and some silverware, too. Except for dishes, there aren't really too many other things we'll need to buy right at first."

They would begin painting the very next day, Whit continued, and should be practically finished with the chore by the time Rog and Pete Kramer arrived. Jackie, delighted by his enthusiasm, realized that she hadn't seen him in such high spirits since the evening of Greg's disappearance. Wistfully, her thoughts turned to Val, and she offered a silent prayer that her friend, too, would soon have something to be happy about.

During the last week before the wedding was scheduled to take place, preparations for the ceremony and the reception became even more frenzied. Greg's parents telephoned daily from San Francisco. Disconsolate at their son's continued absence, even they had begun to urge a postponement. But Val remained adamant, and the house teemed with friends and relatives from sunrise to twilight, to say nothing of the procession of tradespeople connected with the wedding who darted continuously in and out.

At work, too, Jackie found herself buried with chores, but she felt no resentment since the entire staff was engaged in a Herculean effort to boost the *Courier* to a top-ranking position again. To everyone's delight (except the employees of the *Herald*), the circulation figures had continued to skyrocket up ward.

Jackie was poring over a second redraft of the daily "Neighborhood Notes" column on Thursday afternoon when she became aware of a hushed expectancy in the City Room. The ratcheting of typewriters had subsided to a mere occasional pecking sound, and looking up, she saw the other staff members all straining toward the partition which separated Mr. MacFarland's private office from the rest of the room.

Angry voices filtered through the transom.

"Laddie buck, ye're nae better than the rest of us!" Bruce MacFarland ordinarily kept the burr of his Scotch accent under control, but now he had lapsed into a brogue thicker than porridge.

With a start, Jackie recognized Lance Shelby's usually suave voice snap a reply.

"I'm telling you for the last time — I am not a sports hack! If you don't want to depend on the wire service for coverage of that golf tournament, you can go cover it yourself!"

There was a stunned silence.

"You're fired!" roared the editor.

"Oh, no," Lance sneered. "My contract has a year to run. And it doesn't stipulate anything about running off to Tucson to watch a bunch of amateurs sink putts!"

He stalked out of the office, slamming the door with an explosive crack that rattled the windows. Moving like a whirlwind, he snatched his hat off its hook and stormed into the hall so forcefully that papers fluttered off desks in his wake.

The staff members lowered their heads and pretended to be absorbed in their work. Jackie, too, feigned interest in the copy before her, but she slanted her eyes in Melinda's direction.

Looks as if the mighty have fallen, she thought, seeing the look of shock and repugnance which the Society Editor did not bother to disguise. She has finally seen through that Adonis-like façade of his and taken a good look at Lance Shelby.

"What a rotten way for him to act!" Melinda exclaimed. "Every last one of us is working like a coolie to save the *Courier* from bankruptcy, and he's too important to cover a golf tournament!"

Jackie couldn't repress a giggle. "That torch sure went out with a fizzle!"

Melinda blushed. "It certainly did," she said emphatically. "It's high time I let my arm down and stop making like Lady Liberty. To think of all the months I've spent daydreaming about that overgrown kindergartner!"

Lance did not reappear that afternoon, nor did Mr. MacFarland emerge from his private cubicle. Whispered speculation spread among the newspaper's personnel. The *Courier*, finally on the upgrade, could ill afford to lose the prestige of Lance Shelby's famous by-line. Neither could Bruce MacFarland weaken and excuse the star reporter's insubordination. A boiling feud seemed imminent.

Despite the excitement, the day couldn't pass quickly enough to suit Jackie. She was eager to get home and change her clothes. Whit was coming to the Prescott house for dinner and bringing his newly discharged buddies. Felipe, she learned later, had also been invited. He had shyly declined, however, saying that he preferred to stay aboard the *Albatross* and fix himself a plate of *refritos*.

She took an immediate liking to Roger Nelson, whose puppylike friendliness soon also endeared him to Val's parents. Pete

Kramer, too, was a likable young man. He was only sorry, he said, that a job waiting for him in Wyoming prevented his buying into partnership with Whit and Rog.

"Felipe and I finished painting the decks this morning," Whit proudly told Jackie. "Wait until you see that old houseboat now. She's as pert and pretty as a girl of nineteen!"

Val was a quiet spectator to their fun. The wedding had been scheduled to take place at noon on Sunday. With less than three days remaining, every minute had become an ordeal. Jackie felt tears well in her own eyes when the unhappy girl excused herself soon after dinner. How much more of this suspense could Val endure?

Roger and Pete did not need much urging to start them talking about their adventures in the Far East, and Rog "just happened" to have brought along with him a huge manila envelope of photographs which he had taken at various Oriental ports.

"Told you he was a camera bug," Whit said, with a wink at Jackie. "Don't let him cajole you into looking at any of them, or you'll be stuck here all night!"

"Oh, hush you — you art-hater, you!" Jackie made a good-humored face at Whit and swung back to Rog. "I'd love to see the pictures. You'll have to explain where each one was taken, though, since I never joined the Navy and saw the world."

"Be glad to," Rog responded, delighted to have found such a willing audience.

Jackie soon discovered that, unlike many amateur photographers, Rog had a keen knowledge of composition and lighting effects. She thoroughly enjoyed seeing the snapshots taken in Hawaii and Japan, and even the drab, shell-pocked landscape of Formosa emerged as a land of enchantment.

"We really had a lucky break coming home," Rog said. "The ship's generator developed a kink and we put in at Hong Kong for three days while they repaired it. What a fantastic place! I'm just sorry I couldn't have gotten a few good pictures of Red China, as well."

"Huh!" Pete Kramer snorted. "Be glad you didn't. Tell them about the international incident that nearly got us all killed."

"Real cloak-and-dagger stuff," Rog explained. "At least I think it was. Anyway, a patrol boat caught this fellow trying to sneak across from the Chinese mainland into Hong Kong on a junk. The crew of his boat wasted no time in shooting back. It was like a movie — only those weren't blanks!"

"How exciting!" Jackie gasped. "Where were you while all this was taking place?"

Rog grimaced. "On the *Hudson*'s deck,

164

practically in the line of fire. Got some fair shots of the action, too.

"This happened two or three weeks ago. We had just put to sea again and were headed for Tokyo," Pete added. "That patrol boat and junk couldn't have been more than twenty yards off our starboard bow when the bullets started to fly. I went for the hatch, but this goon almost fell over the side taking pictures."

"Well, let me see them!" Jackie cried.

Rog obligingly handed over the top print.

Just as her fingers closed over it, a clatter of running feet beat a tattoo on the cement walk, and an agitated pounding on the front door brought Whit bounding up. Rog turned and relaxed his grip on the other three snapshots; they dropped into Jackie's lap.

The excited gabble of voices would have diverted her attention, too, had not something astonishing caught her eye. She snatched up the glossy print, staring incredulously at it.

"It couldn't be — could it?" she murmured. A dizzying sequence of thoughts swarmed around in her brain, blotting out all consciousness of the outside world. Sharply, she drew in her breath. "But that might explain everything!"

A firm hand grasped her arm. "Jackie!

165

Aren't you coming with us?"

She stared dazedly up at Whit's grim face. "What?"

"Snap out of your trance and come on," he insisted, tugging. "Someone has made another raid on the *Albatross*!"

Only then did Jackie catch sight of Felipe. The Mexican boy was soaking wet from head to toe. He shifted apologetically from one foot to the other as puddles spread across the throw rug where he stood.

The haste with which she was propelled out the door and down the path erased completely the idea which the snapshot had triggered. The photos fell unnoticed to the floor as she ran to keep pace with the others.

"Felipe had fallen asleep on one of the deck chairs. We'd moved them into the galley while the paint dried outside," Whit explained, while they stumbled down the moonlit trail. "I guess since there weren't any lights showing, the prowler figured no one was aboard. He fell coming up the gangplank and woke Felipe, who dashed out to see what all the commotion was about."

"He nearly catch me. I run real fast and jump over the side," Felipe piped up. "Good thing — he was one big fellow!"

"Do you suppose they're after the blueprints again?" Jackie asked in a voice too low for the others to overhear.

Whit angrily shook his head. "Who knows!"

Sand clung grittily to the still-damp paint where the intruder had walked. Surprisingly, though, it led not to the winch which operated the anchor chain, but to the cabin where the boys had their sleeping accommodations.

Whit halted at the doorway, covering every inch of the cabin. There was no disorder here, nothing except a filmy trail of sand to testify to the fact that the prowler had been real and not a specter out of Felipe's nightmares.

Silently Whit proceeded across the floor, careful not to disturb the telltale grains. They led him unerringly to the closet, and while the others poised on the sill ready to leap to his assistance, he flung open the door.

"Nobody here," he announced, his tone a mixture of relief and disappointment.

"Is anything missing?" Jackie called.

Whit searched. Five minutes later, he turned to face them, wearing an expression of acute bewilderment.

"Greg's uniform," he said. "It's gone!"

CHAPTER ELEVEN

Jouncing sleepily along in the bus the next morning, Jackie yawned and tried to prod her unco-operative brain into producing a clear pattern of thoughts. Her present befuddled condition was admittedly her own fault. After all the excitement of the previous evening, she had not succeeded in falling asleep until long past her usual bedtime. And tonight, with the wedding rehearsal to be gotten through — somehow — without the groom, would probably be worse.

Jackie yawned again and straightened her shoulders, forcing herself to wakefulness. What a horrid, mixed-up muddle the situation had become! The events of the night before had only served to deepen the mystery.

The prowler, as was to be expected, had made good his escape well before she and the boys rushed up the gangplank and found the trail of sand leading straight to the closet. Even after a thorough search of the *Albatross*, Whit was insistent that nothing except Greg's

Naval uniform was missing.

"Hat, shoes, tie — the works," she remembered him saying.

"If I were any sort of a detective, that would probably furnish me with a clue," she told herself. "Right now, I feel like Dumb Dora. Nothing makes sense!"

The bus lurched to a stop and a passenger boarded the vehicle. Another tourist, Jackie thought absently, noting the camera carrying case slung across his shoulder. Santa Teresa was becoming popular with summer visi— Suddenly, something clicked inside her head. The sight of the camera had jarred loose a fact that she had been unwittingly carrying around in her benumbed brain for the past eleven hours.

"I'm the world's prize dope!" Jackie exclaimed. "How could I have forgotten anything so important?"

The only excuse she could offer was that Whit had rushed her down the trail before she had time fully to comprehend the evidence revealed by the innocent-looking snapshot. The headlong chase, combined with Felipe's excited testimony and the bewildering disappearance of Greg's uniform, had mired the tiny but oh, so vital fact in her subconscious.

Her first impulse was to leap off the bus and scurry for the nearest telephone. Seeing that

169

she was only a few blocks from the *Courier* building, however, she abandoned this wild idea. She had to think and, for once, to think coherently.

Mr. Quinn would be the logical person to tell, of course. But supposing she were wrong? Supposing the face in the snapshot belonged to someone other than the person she thought it did? She had, after all, examined the picture for a very short time. A too-hasty accusation could result in a lawsuit for slander!

I don't dare make a mistake, she thought feverishly. I must talk to Whit. He'll know what to do.

But this task was not easily accomplished. There was no way of communicating with Whit except through the Prescotts, and her frantic attempts to telephone home were met by the unbroken peal of a bell tolling through an empty house.

"Val said something about going down to the church to arrange for the rehearsal," Jackie recalled, pouncing on the directory. She *had* to reach Whit!

"Say, are you coming or not?" Ted Rigney asked peevishly, appearing in the doorway. "I've been waiting downstairs for twenty minutes."

With a sinking heart, Jackie remembered the "inquiring reporter" column. Should she fake illness, return home and try to contact Whit personally? She caught the stern eye of Bruce MacFarland, and wilted. Best not to chance it. Heaven only knew where Whit might be, anyway, with two friends newly arrived in town.

"Sorry," she mumbled to Ted, reaching for her notebook. Another hour's delay couldn't make that much difference.

Jackie went mechanically through the routine of stopping pedestrians, identifying herself and asking the "question of the day." Although she dutifully recorded the replies in neat shorthand squiggles, her mind was racing along on a track of its own. *Could* she have mistaken that face? Was *he* the person who had collaborated with the Chinese Communists — or was the man in the snapshot some total stranger? When she sat down to transcribe her notes, not a word on the page looked familiar.

The noon whistle sounded, and for the tenth time Jackie dialed the Prescotts' number. No response. Where could they *be?*

Standing in line at the cafeteria counter, all of her indecision faded and the questions she had asked herself again and again were suddenly resolved. Her eyes riveted on a man on the other side of the room. His face and the face of the man in the snapshot were identical. She was positive!

But — proof? Was the evidence of a lone snapshot taken halfway across the world strong enough to warrant the serious accusations of kidnapping and theft? And . . . espionage?

For a half minute, Jackie wavered. Perhaps she could force a damaging admission from him. A surprise question might turn the trick. Then, reluctantly, she shook her head.

"This isn't a court of law. It would still be just his word against mine, and if I say anything now, I'll put him on his guard," she decided. "I had better leave the quizzing to an expert."

About to abandon her lunch tray and dash back upstairs to the telephone, Jackie felt a strong masculine hand clamp down on her shoulder.

"Oh! Ted, you startled me," she choked.

"Oops, didn't mean to spill your soup. Guess I'm a little overexuberant this afternoon." The cameraman's homely face was a wreath of smiles. "Have I got news! Jackie, it's the greatest thing that ever happened to me. Let's sit over here. I want to tell Lance about it, too."

"No, really I —"

"Come on!"

Her protest completely ignored, she had no

choice but to allow herself to be led along. Already several people in the cafeteria had turned to stare in their direction.

"I'll phone Mr. Quinn the minute I've finished eating," Jackie promised herself.

Ted clattered his tray down on the table and slid into the booth next to Lance Shelby. "My friend, beside you sits a man whose heart overflows with gratitude," he crowed exultantly.

Lance seemed annoyed by the intrusion. His tone was tinged with frost. "Really?"

"Yes sir, a man whose most cherished dream has at last come true," Ted went on, oblivious to the cool reception. "You did me a tremendous favor yesterday, whether you know it or not. I'm flying out to Tucson tonight to cover that golf tournament — pictures *and* story!"

"Oh, Ted, how wonderful for you!" Jackie cried.

Lance, however, was less generous with his congratulations.

"Glad to hear that our esteemed editor has found someone to do his odd jobs for him," he said scornfully. "Maybe now I'll be free to concentrate on the really important stories." Rising abruptly, he strode away from the table.

Ted gaped after the reporter's fast-retreating back. "For Pete's sake! What ails him?"

"Acid indigestion from the chili con carne, maybe. Don't let him upset you," Jackie said. "Perhaps he resented our barging in on him. He's been awfully moody ever since that battle with Mr. MacFarland."

Hoping to atone for Lance's rudeness, she added, "I didn't know you were a sports writer, as well as a photographer."

Ted flushed with pleasure, the snub forgotten. "I'm not, really. But I am awfully keen on golf, and so are a lot of other people in this town. That's why the Chief is so eager to get first-hand coverage of that tournament. He knows the *Herald* will just carry the usual wire-service reports."

"How to win subscribers and influence circulation!" Jackie finished her salad and stacked the dishes on the tray. "Good luck, Ted. I hate to run off like this, but I have an important phone call to make. Don't forget to duck when they shout 'fore!' "

"Scram, or you'll be ducking," he snorted, but his voice held no animosity. Already he was glancing around for someone else to whom he could confide the good news.

Hurrying into the City Room, Jackie looked quickly about. The entire floor appeared deserted.

Lucky break, she thought, hastening to her desk and snatching up the telephone. Now if only everyone will stay away for another ten minutes —

Her call to the Federal agent's office was answered promptly, but to Jackie's chagrin, she was informed that Mr. Quinn was not at his desk.

"Would you care to speak with someone else?" the switchboard operator asked.

Jackie almost groaned in exasperation. About to refuse, she changed her mind.

"Yes, yes, anyone. It's extremely urgent!"

The agent to whom the call was transferred was unknown to Jackie. She spoke rapidly but concisely, aware of the need to relay the message before being interrupted. At any moment, the other *Courier* personnel would begin trickling back from lunch.

"This is Jacqueline Torrance. Mr. Quinn has been investigating the disappearance of an ex-Naval lieutenant, Gregory Malden. Tell him — tell him please that I've discovered something terribly vital to the case. It ties in with an illegal trip to Red China —"

A floor board behind her creaked warningly. Jackie flung a look over her shoulder. Was someone standing behind that partition? If the wrong person should overhear —

"It isn't safe for me to talk any longer," she whispered into the mouthpiece. "Tell Mr. Quinn I'll call him later."

Jackie dropped the receiver onto the hook and started toward the back of the room, bent on investigating that telltale creak. Before she had gone a dozen feet, her progress was halted by Bruce MacFarland's entrance.

"Oh, Miss Torrance," the editor called. "Run this batch of copy down to 'Advertising,' will you? Jim will know what to do about it."

She would never really be certain, Jackie thought, speeding downstairs on the errand. It was possible that someone had entered through one of the rear doors while she was intent upon her phone call. She didn't really think so — but just the same, she was glad she had not chanced saying anything further.

Jackie's resolve to call the Federal agent's office again within a few minutes was destined to be thwarted. Her desk was stacked high with work, and whenever a brief breathing space did occur, either Melinda or one of the other staff members was hovering within earshot. Nor were there any errands which took her out of the office so that she could relay her message from the privacy of a telephone booth.

It was nearly three ·o'clock before her opportunity came. Jackie reached for the receiver, but just as her fingers closed over the instrument, it rang.

"Miss Torrance," she answered.

"Are you the lady who advertised for an apartment?" a male voice inquired.

"Oh! Yes, I am," she said, but not too eagerly. This one would probably turn out like the other responses to her ad — too expensive for Croesus.

"We have a very nice apartment which has just been vacated. It is attached to a house, but you would have your own private entrance. Nice sunny bedroom, bath, kitchen, and living room. The furnishings are practically new."

It sounded ideal! Determined to remain calm, Jackie asked, "What is the rental price?"

The sum he quoted was as attractive as the appartment's description. He cleared his throat, sounding a trifle embarrassed. "I should mention that there are two or three other parties interested in the apartment. They are coming out to look it over this evening."

And she couldn't possibly go anywhere tonight! The first reasonable offer she'd had, and it turned up on the day of Val's wedding rehearsal. Maybe, though —

Jackie flashed a look at the clock. There might be a chance yet. If she left now, she could see the apartment and still arrive home early.

"I'll be there as soon as I can," she promised.

"Fine," the man replied heartily.

Vaguely, Jackie wondered at the note of relief in his voice. No doubt it was a tedious job, finding just the right tenant for a vacancy. She jotted down the address on her desk pad, tore off the sheet and tucked it into her purse. The original purpose of her reach toward the phone was completely jolted out of her mind by this wonderful find.

Permission to leave work early was granted more readily than she had anticipated. Hastening out of the *Courier* building, Jackie debated about whether or not to take a taxi. It would be quicker, but also a good deal more expensive. There had been so many unexpected expenses connected with the wedding that she hesitated to put a further strain on her budget. Then, taking another look at the address, she remembered having seen the street name while riding to work in the morning. It couldn't be more than a few blocks off the regular bus line, she reasoned. To cement the argument, no taxis were in sight, while a bus was now rumbling up to the curb. Jackie hopped aboard.

The bus deposited her at the corner of Tolver and Larkin, and Jackie, turning up Tolver, discovered that the block was numbered 800. The apartment she sought was at 26 Tolver Street.

"Cheapskate — you should have taken the cab," she berated herself, doggedly setting out on the trek.

Fortunately, the street slanted gently downhill most of the way. A leisurely ocean breeze wafted a scent of salt through the air, and Jackie realized that the house must be very near the sea. Her excitement mounted. A marine view, in addition to the promised sunny rooms!

Two or three blocks later, she entered one of the town's best residential areas. She recognized the crossstreet names as addresses of several wealthy persons whose pictures often decorated the *Courier*'s society pages.

Goodness! In this neighborhood you're practically undressed without a mink coat. Why should anyone who lives around here be taking in roomers? Jackie wondered.

Quickly reminding herself that it was possible for the rich as well as the poor to encounter hard times, she strolled on. The urge to linger and admire the palatial residences surrounded by their luxuriously land-

179

scaped grounds was highly tempting. Only the remembrance of the wedding rehearsal prompted her to hasten her steps.

Number 26 Tolver Street *was* near the sea. In fact, it was the last house on the block, separated from the shore line only by a concrete abutment and its own well-groomed lawns. Her pulses pounding with anticipation, Jackie tripped up the flagstone walk and mounted the steps.

The door swung open, even before the first melodious peal of chimes had faded away. Jackie stepped inside, squinting a bit in the dim light. Coming up the walk, she had paid little notice to the blank appearance of the windows. Now, as she advanced into the entrance hall, she realized that the shutters were closed.

To her left was a large room, a parlor of sorts. But — the furniture! It was all swathed in dust sheets. The massive chairs hunched whitely around a low table, like spirits attending a ghostly tea party.

Fear struck Jackie. It rose wildly in her throat, and she choked back a desire to scream. Everything about this place was dreadfully wrong!

"I — I'm sorry; I d-don't think this location would be suitable for me," she managed to stammer to the man who, except for sweeping shut the door as she entered, had not moved or spoken.

He lumbered closer, a hulking giant, taller and broader than anyone she had ever seen. As he stepped forward into what murky light filtered through to the hall, Jackie's skin prickled into goose pimples.

That face! Distorted now by a gleeful smirk, his craggy brow and nose and chin completely overshadowed the small, beady eyes. She had seen him before somewhere, she felt sure. It seemed terribly important that she remember where.

But more important was the need to escape, to get away from this cavernous dungeon and its awesome caretaker. The hall's width provided ample room for maneuvering. Jackie edged backward, pivoting in an arc away from the man and toward the door. Panic surged anew as he advanced. Her fingers, stretched taut behind her back, made contact with the door and fumbled for the knob.

She risked a fleeting look over her shoulder, removing her eyes from the giant just long enough to fix the location of the knob firmly in her mind. The next instant her hand closed over it, twisting, wrenching. Futilely. Although she tugged with all her might, the heavy door refused to budge.

"Now, ain't that a shame?" the man observed. "Locked, ain't it?"

Jackie, recognizing defeat, let her arm drop to her side. "Let me out of here at once!"

"Shucks, you just came. Ain't you even going to stay for tea?" A hoarse chuckle rattled in his throat. "You don't want to hurt the boss's feelings by running off before he gets here, do you?"

"Now look —" About to embark on a tirade, Jackie broke off with a sharp intake of breath. Recollection came flooding back as his jutting features reverted to their natural belligerent cast. Of course that was where she had seen him — not personally, but through the lens of Don's camera!

"You're Buck Younger!"

His jaw slacked. "Hey — how'd you know?"

"I got acquainted with your picture the last time I bought stamps." This wasn't the case, but it might have been. Certainly no more villainous-looking "Wanted" poster had ever embellished the walls of a post office.

A furious rush of blood mottled his face. "Don't get cute, sister," he growled. Rough fingers tightened over her wrist. "Go on — get up the stairs!"

Half-dragged, half-pushed by the Navy deserter, Jackie was forced up the stairway and shoved into a small sitting room at the back of the house.

In spite of her terror, she couldn't help noticing the tasteful furnishings. What on earth was Buck Younger doing in a beautiful home like this? Fugitives, she suspected, usually went to earth in isolated and much more sordid surroundings.

She promptly dismissed the question when a muffled thud from the adjacent room shattered the silence. So she wasn't the only prisoner in this house!

Jackie took a shot in the dark.

"What have you done with Greg Malden?"

Younger's eyes narrowed to mere peepholes in his weatherbeaten skin. "You're too smart for your own good. Shut up!"

Obediently Jackie subsided, pretending to cringe against the back of the chair. If he believed her to be thoroughly cowed, he might become careless. He couldn't just sit there forever, glowering at her.

I've got to get Greg out of here, as well as myself, she thought, mulling over the possible chances for escape. At least it's something to know he is still alive!

Arranging for Greg's release would be even more difficult than breaking away herself. Apparently he was well confined, probably even bound and gagged, since the single thud was the only indication of his presence he had been able to give. If only she had time to work out a plan!

Buck Younger had at first settled himself near the door, but as the minutes ticked by, he began to show signs of restlessness. Again and again, he consulted his watch, shaking his head and muttering under his breath.

He's waiting for someone, Jackie thought, suddenly recalling his mention of the "boss."

She knew now that the telephone call had been a carefully planned ruse, designed to decoy her away from the office before she had an opportunity to speak again with the Federal agent. How gullible she had been not to realize that sooner. In failing to call Mr. Quinn, she had tossed away the only clue to Greg's whereabouts — and her own, now, as well.

She was almost considering a desperation leap through the window when a door thudded shut in the lower regions of the house and footsteps creaked up the stairway.

In another moment, Jackie stood face to face with the traitor who had spirited away the blueprints from Port Dixon, the man who had masterminded Greg's kidnapping and her own.

"Well, well, little fly. How nice of you to come into my parlor!"

Lance Shelby flung back his head and roared with laughter.

CHAPTER TWELVE

Lance continued to laugh as he crossed the threshold. He seemed highly entertained by the situation.

"So you *are* the one!" Jackie breathed. "I thought so, but I couldn't quite believe that someone I knew and worked with could turn out to be a — a turncoat!"

Lance quirked an amused eyebrow at his companion. "Such fire! What have you been telling our guest, Buck?"

"I ain't said a word," Younger disclaimed. "She had it all figured out. Recognized me right off and then asked about that guy in there." Nervously, he jerked his head toward the next room. "Gee, boss, I think we'd better clear out of here."

"Now don't start getting excited," Lance told him. "Nothing is going wrong this time. By tomorrow —"

"By tomorrow you'll both be in jail where you belong!" Jackie burst out. "The FBI knows all about your double life!"

Lance's expression hardened. "May I remind you that your telephone call was never completed? I'll admit it was a shock, standing there in the City Room and hearing you mention Red China, but I tricked you into leaving the building before you could make any really damaging statements. As you have probably guessed, it was Buck who called you about the apartment — after I had written out such a glowing description that you couldn't possibly resist coming to see it for yourself."

Coolly, he lit a cigarette. "Let's not waste time fencing. You are in no position to bandy insults with me. On the other hand, I can easily arrange your release — if you tell me exactly what I want to know."

"I shan't tell you anything!"

"How did you know I had visited the Chinese mainland?"

Jackie clenched her fists and said nothing. Whatever happened, she must not mention the snapshot!

"I abhor violence, but I am afraid that if you persist in being stubborn, your friend Mr. Malden will pay the penalty," Lance prompted icily. "He is in no condition to withstand much of Buck's — persuasion, shall we say? Buck, you may —"

Greg had endured enough! "You were seen," Jackie said faintly.

"Ridiculous! By whom? A harbor full of illiterate fishermen?" Then a possibility hit him. He jerked around suddenly and flung a question at Buck. "The *Hudson* — has she made port yet?"

"Yeah, late last week. But what's that got to do with —"

"So some of your sailor friend's buddies have been reminiscing about their adventures in Kowloon Bay? That could be an unfortunate coincidence, but apparently their tales made little impression on anyone else, or I'd have heard from the authorities before this."

Despite his assured manner, Jackie felt certain that the information had upset him. An ugly twitch dragged at the corner of his mouth. He wouldn't be so worried, she thought with a gulp, if he knew how slim the evidence against him really was!

Abruptly, Lance wheeled, hurling an order over his shoulder. "Lock her in there with him and come downstairs. We may have to speed up our plans."

Younger jumped to obey, shoving Jackie ahead of him and clamping her arm in an iron grip while unbolting the door of the adjacent room. The next instant she was thrust rudely forward. Before she could regain her balance, the bolt was again shot into place, and Buck's lumbering footsteps echoed down the hall.

"Greg!" Jackie cried, dropping to her knees in front of Greg, who was bound hand and foot to a chair. With a swift motion, she tore the twisted gag from his mouth. "Am I glad to see you!"

He made a rueful attempt to grin. "I wish I could say the same. How did *you* get involved in this mess?"

"It's a long story; I'll tell you later." Hurrying to the back of the chair, Jackie began to pluck at the knots that laced his hands. "Have you any idea of what those two crooks are up to?"

Greg groaned. "They managed to get hold of my uniform and I.D. cards. They've threatened to harm Val unless I co-operate in helping them steal something from the Port Dixon base."

Whit's guess had been right! Jackie thought. That pair of traitors intended to make off with the revolutionary new radar instrument. What sheer audacity! And their plan might still be successful!

She seemed to be making no headway with the knots. Ignoring a broken fingernail, she continued her struggle with the cruelly tied rope.

"This is the strangest hideout I've ever seen," she said. "Who owns it? Do you know?"

"A wealthy couple who are vacationing in South America. I heard Shelby bragging about the way he'd tricked the caretaker into lending him the key long enough to make a wax impression of it."

"Guess he figured the police would never suspect Buck Younger of hiding in a plush neighborhood like this." Jackie grimaced. Was there nothing Lance Shelby had overlooked? "Does anyone ever come here?" she asked hopefully.

"Just a fellow who cuts the grass every few days. I tried to signal him from the window once, but it was no go. Those heavy screens are practically armorplated!" A thought struck Greg. "The blueprints — are they safe?"

"Yes, thanks to your inspiration about the anchor chain." There! His hands were free. "How did you manage to keep the new hiding place a secret?" Jackie asked, turning her efforts to the cords that bound his feet.

Greg laughed outright. "I convinced Shelby that I'd mailed them back to the admiral. Was he furious! Good thing he didn't ask which mailbox I used — there isn't one within blocks of Val's house."

Greg was free now, but the rope burns on his wrists and ankles were extremely painful. Their combined efforts to restore circulation

189

to his benumbed limbs made him wince.

"Is there any chance —" he had started to ask, when heavy footsteps clomped down the hall and paused outside the door. Before Jackie had time to more than blink, Lance Shelby and Buck Younger had entered the room.

To her astonishment, Lance was outfitted from head to foot in a smart Naval uniform. By the clever use of make-up, he had even altered his features, so that he now bore a superficial resemblance to Greg.

"Surprised?" Lance chuckled. "We've decided to dispense with your services, Lieutenant. I'm afraid that once we got to Port Dixon patriotism might blunder into the way of your better interests. Your interference has cost us enough already."

"You won't get away with this!" Greg cried angrily. Forgetting his weakened condition, he leaped toward Shelby, only to pitch forward when his ankles buckled beneath him.

"What a hero!" Buck jeered in derision.

Jackie offered a helping hand as Greg limped back to the chair. "I don't see how you can stand to live with yourself!" she blazed at Shelby.

"Money helps," he acknowledged. "I expect to live very well indeed, once this transaction goes through. No more debts, no more people hounding me to pay the rent, or threatening to repossess my car —"

"The richest kid on the block!"

"And the smartest, don't forget. You and Mr. Malden were no match for me. And remember what happened to Alexei Litvinov when he tried to steal the blueprints, instead of meeting my price!" His laugh had an ugly sound. "Comrade Litvinov's Red Chinese counterpart was only too happy to accept my offer."

Jackie turned away in disgust. The window, although tightly bolted, offered a comforting glimpse of the normal outside world. The late afternoon sun sparkled across trees and shrubbery. Down the street, she supposed, people were going about their daily routine, completely unaware of the threat this unscrupulous man and his companion posed to their country.

Suddenly, from the side of the house, a sputtering racket arose to rupture the suburban quiet. The next minute, a gardener pushing a power lawnmower came into her line of vision. Jackie craned her neck as he passed directly beneath the window. Hopeful at first to gain his attention, her half-raised arm dropped when she caught sight of his face. How in the world —

"Get away from the window!" Lance

snarled, leaping toward her.

Buck pinioned her arms, shoving her back from the window while he glanced down. "It's just that old geezer with the lawn-mower," he said nonchalantly.

Jackie's frantic efforts to break free were quickly subdued. "What are we going to do with this little wildcat?" Buck puffed.

"Tie her up — him too," Lance ordered. "We'll leave them here for the Merritts to find when they return from Buenos Aires next month." He frowned at his watch. "Hurry up! I have to make it through the Port Dixon gate by nine o'clock —"

Buck stooped, reaching for a length of rope coiled on the floor. For a split second his grip slackened. Wrenching loose, Jackie sprinted toward the door and yanked it open.

"Help! Mr. Quinn, help!" she screamed, eluding Shelby's desperation grab that ripped her sleeve.

She had raced less than halfway down the hall when, with a thunderous crash, the front door burst open. A grim-faced team of Federal agents, followed by an agitated-looking young man with bright-red hair, swarmed into the house and up the stairs.

"Oh, Whit, I've never been so glad to see anyone in my life!" Jackie sobbed as he caught her up in his arms.

When, a moment or two later, Jackie accompanied by Whit re-entered the room which for two weeks had been Greg's prison, they found that the Government men had already snapped handcuffs on Lance Shelby and Buck Younger. Surly and disgruntled, they were led away to a waiting police van.

One of the men, dressed in an old shirt and trousers and wearing a battered gardener's hat, looked oddly unlike a Federal agent.

"Mr. Quinn, do you always keep a spare wardrobe on hand for odd jobs?" Jackie asked him, after she had expressed her gratitude for the timeliness of his arrival.

"In my line of work you run into all sorts of odd jobs," he said, poker-faced. A twinkle brushed his eyes. "Like rescuing damsels in distress. The act with the lawnmower accomplished our purpose — we drew their attention to the back of the house until the rest of our men were in position to rush the front."

"But how did you ever find us?" she wondered.

Whit grinned. "An old pencil and paper trick our friend here knows led us to you."

Mr. Quinn explained. "My colleague contacted me as soon as he had finished talking to you. He had an idea you might be in some sort of trouble." Even he was forced to smile at the understatement. "Unfortunately, you had already left the newspaper office by the time we arrived there. The scratch-pad on your desk gave us the clue we needed. The top sheet was blank but marred with indentations. By rubbing a pencil lightly over these marks, we brought out a tracing of an address — twenty-six Tolver Street."

"Shelby's one little oversight," Greg remarked. "He thought of everything else. By the time —"

"The time! Heavens, what time *is* it?" Jackie cried. "We have a wedding rehearsal to attend!"

Several hours later, a jubilant group gathered in the Prescotts' living room.

"It's so *good* to have you home safe again," Val bubbled, squeezing her fiancé's hand.

"Believe me, it's good to be here," responded Greg with just as much fervor. His two-week incarceration had left him looking tired and several pounds thinner, but aside from the ugly rope burns on his wrists and ankles, he was none the worse for his experience.

"Sorry I had to run out on our appointment, sir," he apologized to Mr. Quinn. "Those characters grabbed me on the way back to the *Albatross*. I tried to play for time, but they were in an ugly mood after discovering that the blueprints were gone. Buck knocked me cold, and when I came to I was tied up in the house on Tolver Street."

"You did a fine job, son," the Federal agent said gruffly. "You and this young lady both, although she might have been a little less impetuous when it came to apartment hunting." He turned his keen eyes on Jackie. "Tell me, what gave you the idea that Lance Shelby was involved in the kidnapping?"

"I guess I really knew when I saw that snapshot Rog Nelson took. Though even then, I could hardly believe it."

"Roy Nelson!" Whit exclaimed. "But — he just arrived from the Orient a couple of days ago."

"Believe it or not, the clue to the whole affair came from Hong Kong. Remember, he and Pete were telling about the clash between that Chinese junk and the patrol boat in Kowloon Bay? The man attempting to slip quietly back to Hong Kong was Lance Shelby. The incident delayed him long enough to cause him to miss his plane — and it took place in full view of the men aboard the *Hudson.*" She smiled teasingly. "Don't you ever dare say another disparaging word about camera bugs. If Rog hadn't braved Tommy-gun bullets to take those pictures, we might

195

never have figured out a solution to this mystery!"

"Have Younger and Shelby signed a confession yet, sir?" Greg asked.

Mr. Quinn nodded. "They saw it was no use trying to deny anything — not after we'd actually caught them red-handed. Each of them is doing his best to throw most of the blame on the other in hopes of being allowed to turn State's evidence and get off with a lighter sentence. It's up to a judge and jury, of course, but I feel certain they will both receive maximum prison terms."

"I'm still wondering how the two of them came to team up," Whit puzzled. "They had nothing in common."

"Younger told us about that," Mr. Quinn explained. "Seems that a couple of months ago he got into a water-front brawl. His opponent wound up in the hospital, seriously injured. The police didn't manage to discover Younger's identity, but Lance Shelby witnessed the whole affair. He got in touch with Buck a few days later — threatened to tip off the authorities unless Younger agreed to co-operate with him."

A cold tremor ran up Jackie's spine. Such utter ruthlessness! Lance had balked at nothing where achievement of his ambitions was concerned. He had even jeopardized his job on the *Courier* by refusing to take on the Tucson golf assignment when it threatened to interfere with his plans for returning one last time to Port Dixon.

"Even Don — his own friend," she murmured. "Lance nearly fractured his skull to prevent anyone from seeing that negative. And then he had the nerve to visit him in the hospital!"

"Probably checking up to make sure he wasn't recognized," Mr. Quinn surmised, getting to his feet.

Clad once again in his usual somber gray hat and suit, it was difficult for Jackie to visualize him as he had appeared that afternoon. What an effective disguise those tattered old gardening clothes had made. Her faith in Thomas J. Quinn had not been misplaced!

"You must be sure to come to our wedding," Val told Mr. Quinn as she and Greg escorted the Federal agent to the door. "Sunday afternoon — don't forget."

Mr. Quinn *had* come, Jackie noticed with pleasure as she left the receiving line to mingle with the guests. At the moment he was sipping punch and chatting with her parents in a corner of the room.

Pausing to admire the three-tiered wedding cake which formed the centerpiece of the

197

beautifully decorated buffet table, Jackie thought how fortunate it was that her mother and father had known nothing of her brief kidnapping until she was safely back with her friends.

Lucky, too, she thought, that they had taken such an immediate liking to Whit. While they regretted Jackie's decision to leave college and continue with her job on the *Courier*, they agreed that their daughter was mature enough to select the way of life she preferred.

"I can see the obvious attractions of Santa Teresa," Mrs. Torrance had said, following a mother and daughter tête-à-tête on Saturday. "Such a nice young man! I'm sure he will make you very happy, dear."

"Don't post the banns yet, Mom," Jackie replied with a laugh. "For all I know, he might have decided to bolt back to the peace and quiet of that ranch in Montana!"

But Whit's expression as she joined him now erased this fear. "You make a gorgeous maid of honor," he told her. "Have you ever thought of graduating into the bride class?"

"Occasionally," Jackie confessed.

She was spared a further admission when Mr. Prescott clapped his hands and requested everyone's attention. An expectant hush settled over the reception guests as Val, clutching her long train in one hand and her bridal bouquet in the other, ascended the first half-dozen steps of the staircase.

"All you unwed lassies — front and center!" she called gaily.

"Better go ahead while you're still eligible," Whit teased, urging Jackie forward.

With Fran Harris and a score of other girls, she took her place at the foot of the stairs. She thought she saw one of Val's eyelids flutter downward in a wink. Then, with a cry of "Catch!" the new Mrs. Malden tossed the fragrant mass of orange blossoms straight into Jackie's outstretched fingers. Amid an envious chorus of "oohs" and "ahs," she bore the token proudly back to Whit.

"I think Val has been reading my mind," he said with a grin. "Your catching that thing sort of ties in with an idea I've been working on. Since you're not prone to seasickness, I believe I have the ideal solution to your housing problem. Care to hear about it?"

Jackie tightened her hold on the orange blossoms. "I'd love to hear about it!" she said.

We hope you have enjoyed this Large Print book. Other Thorndike Press or Chivers Press Large Print books are available at your library or directly from the publishers.

For more information about current and upcoming titles, please call or write, without obligation, to:

Thorndike Press
P.O. Box 159
Thorndike, Maine 04986 USA
Tel. (800) 257-5157

OR

Chivers Press Limited
Windsor Bridge Road
Bath BA2 3AX
England
Tel. (0225) 335336

All our Large Print titles are designed for easy reading, and all our books are made to last.